A Woman Named Anne

A Woman Named Anne

Henry Cecil

Academy
Chicago
Publishers

Published in 1993 by
Academy Chicago Publishers
363 West Erie Street
Chicago, Illinois 60610

Library of Congress Cataloging-in Publication Data

Cecil, Henry, 1902-1976.
     A woman named anne / by Henry Cecil
        p.   cm.
      ISBN 0-89733-338-1
      I. Title.
  PR6053.E3W6   1990
   823'.914—dc20
                            90-32734
                               CIP

A Woman Named Anne

Mr. Ringmer could not contain himself. He turned to his client, who was sitting next to him, and whispered:

"What did I tell you? He's got her tied up in the first question."

"Silence," said the usher.

Mr. Ringmer, slightly red in the face, turned his head round as though to see who the offender was. But the strong North Country voice of the judge checked him in the middle of his pantomime.

"That won't do, Mr. Ringmer," said His Honor Judge Brace. "It was you. If you want to talk, please go outside."

It was 1960 and they were sitting in one of the small rooms at the Law Courts which had been converted into a court. So anxious was everyone—Parliament, the legal authorities, many of the judges, and the public—that divorces should take place as fast as possible that almost every available room in the Law Courts had been converted into a court. In these rooms County Court judges, sitting temporarily as judges of the Divorce Division of the High Court, tried divorce cases, although apparently the cases were too important to be tried by them in their capacity of County Court judges. But how right the authorities were. They knew. A County Court judge sitting in his little County Court in Slatterbury and called "Your Honor" was one thing, but the same judge sitting in the High Court and called "my lord" was quite another. Position made the man. In fact Judge Brace was quite fit to have been appointed a High Court judge. Few judges of any rank had a swifter intelligence. He was rarely wrong and rarely upset on appeal, even when he was right. He had, however, other qualities which, though attractive to some practitioners, did not endear him to others. He did not like pomp or ceremony. He was a down-to-earth judge. He could be extremely colloquial in his language and in criticizing an argument he sometimes used expressions which were resented.

The room in which the case was being tried was extremely small. The judge's chair was on a small dais and below him at a desk sat the official called "the associate." But, though the judge was seated above the rows where solicitors, counsel, witnesses, and the public sat, they were all very close to each other. Mr. Ringmer ought to have realized that. The judge, although not worrying in the least whether the public stood up when he left the court or if counsel called him "Your Honor" instead of "My Lord," did not like unnecessary noise during the proceedings.

Mr. Ringmer looked red and sheepish but all the same he was not sorry that Judge Brace was trying the case. If it had to be a County Court judge, he could think of none whom he would have preferred. Mr. Ringmer was an efficient solicitor with a flair for choosing the right man for the job. If he could have been allowed to choose not only the counsel but also the judges for his cases he would have won even more of them. Seventy-five percent of cases would be decided in the same way by any judge, however good the advocacy on one side and however bad on the other. But 25 percent is a considerable proportion and, if one in four cases can go wrong when it ought to go right, a great deal depends upon the knowledge, experience, and ability of the solicitor in charge. By choosing the right counsel he has gone a long way toward winning his client's case, if capable of being won. And if it was not capable of being won, Mr. Ringmer would not normally have allowed his client to fight it.

The nonlawyer might be forgiven for complaining that,

if one out of four cases may be decided in the wrong way, it is not justice. Who said it was? Mankind can only aim at justice and, being fallible, must of necessity miss the mark from time to time. Some lawyers might say that 75 percent was too low a figure for cases which ended as they should have ended, a few might say it was too high. But no experienced lawyer would dispute that at the very best the result of 10 percent of all cases tried may be the wrong one. When you are dealing with such a precious commodity as justice a mistake in one case out of ten may seem horrifying. But you could say the same about doctors or surveyors, not to mention motorists. Human justice will never be perfect even with the use of law reformers, ombudsmen, and computers; even if you fuse the professions of solicitor and barrister; even if Parliamentary draftsmen are compelled to write in simple, intelligible English; even if judges have fewer holidays. Whatever improvements may be made, there will always be some injustice and, when you lose the crossroad collision case where, if it's the last thing you say, you know you should have won if there were any justice in the world, don't go home and commit suicide or write a rude letter to the judge but console yourself with the thought that there was one injustice which you did not suffer—you were not killed in the accident.

The cross-examination continued.

"Would you be good enough to answer the question, madam? Why have you not committed adultery with Mr. Amberley?"

"Because I haven't wanted to," said Anne.

"Then you would have if you'd wanted to?"

Delicious, thought Mr. Ringmer, and he looked interestedly at Anne. What was the right answer? What would he reply if he were in the witness box? Supposing he had wanted to sleep with a woman, why would he not have done so? Well, he knew the answer to that one. His wife. But Anne was a widow.

"Certainly not," said Anne.

"Why not?"

There it was again. Coventry would not let go. He went on like a steamroller until he'd rolled you flat. Mr. Ringmer hoped that his client, Mrs. Amberley, was appreciating the performance. He did not much care for her, but after many years of experience Mr. Ringmer had long ceased to identify himself with his clients. As a young man it is difficult not to do so, particularly if you like the client. And you start with a predisposition to like a new client, as the manager of a hotel is inclined to do, until the customer has complained so often that the only thing he does with pleasure is to deliver the bill. Mrs. Amberley looked about forty-five, was good-looking in a hard sort of way and very smartly dressed. She owned a number of very successful retail dress shops and was one of Mr. Ringmer's wealthier clients. She had been married fifteen years but she suddenly turned her husband out of the house (which belonged to her) and put a detective on permanent watch. In due course evidence was obtained which, if true, showed pretty conclusively that Amberley had committed adultery with Anne. But they denied the charge completely and Amberley had given evidence in support of his denial. He had made a very good impression. The main evidence against him and Anne was that of the detective and, if Anne remained as untouched in cross-examination as Amberley, it was very doubtful indeed if any judge would find the charge proved. So everything really depended on Coventry's smashing Anne.

"Why would you not have slept with Mr. Amberley if you'd wanted to?" persisted Coventry.

"He mightn't have wanted to."

"Supposing he had wanted to?"

This, thought Mr. Ringmer, is like a superb passage in music to a music lover. Each phrase seems better than the last, and all lead up to the final exquisite resolution. Mr. Ringmer wondered what it would be. What *could* the wretched woman say? She was a lovely girl, as old as Mrs. Amberley but so beautiful that Mr. Ringmer had to think of her as a girl. And she stood there in the witness box sensitive and defiant. She was a worthy opponent for Coventry. Mr. Ringmer had felt that she would be even before the case began. Her letters showed that she was highly intelligent or advised by someone who was. And her answers to her own counsel and to the occasional questions from the judge showed that they were her own letters.

"Supposing he had wanted to?" she repeated and gave the ghost of a smile. It made her look more lovely than ever. Whether Coventry was unconsciously affected by the smile or whether it was pure accident, he suddenly let her off that particular hook. Without insisting on a reply he went on:

"Was there no opportunity?"

"That's ridiculous," said Anne, striking back at once when given the chance. Thought Mr. Ringmer, Just like a fighting dog which has been released from the grip of his master.

"What's ridiculous?" asked Coventry.

She was now for the moment dictating the way the struggle should continue.

"Nearly everyone has the opportunity."

"How d'you know?" asked Coventry.

"It's obvious."

"What's obvious?"

"That if people want to sleep together, they can find a way of doing it."

"How do you know?"

"Everyone knows."

"Please assume that his lordship doesn't know," said Coventry, "and tell me how you'd set about it."

Mr. Ringmer, who had been disappointed when Coventry for no apparent reason had lowered his guard and let Anne get the upper hand for a moment, now admired him even more. True, he had let her slip for the moment but here he was back again on top.

"Tell me how you'd set about it." The words sounded happily in Mr. Ringmer's ears.

"Must I answer these offensive questions, my lord?" Anne appealed to the judge.

She's down, thought Mr. Ringmer, and began to count. One—two—three—

"I'm afraid so," said the judge.

"Well, Mrs. Preston," said Coventry, "how *would* you set about it?"

"How on earth can I say, without knowing the circumstances?"

"Let me help you," said Coventry. "The circumstances are that Mr. Amberley is staying in a hotel in the country. You are living alone in a flat in London. You both have cars."

"What is the question?"

"How would you set about committing adultery with Mr. Amberley if you wanted to?"

"I could have taken a room at his hotel."

Splendid, thought Mr. Ringmer. Paragraph six of the petition.

"You could have taken a room at his hotel. Yes. Did you by any chance do that?"

"Yes, I did as a matter of fact. But it was nowhere near his."

"How d'you know that?"

"They were on different floors."

"How do you know?"

"I saw him going up the staircase to the floor above mine."

"He might have been going to a bathroom."

"He had a private bathroom. How do I know? He told me so."

"Was it a nice bathroom?"

"How should I know?"

"He might have told you that too."

"Well, he didn't."

"But he did confide to you that he had a private bathroom. How did he come to mention that?"

"I haven't the faintest idea."

"Would you try to remember, please. You weren't just sitting in the lounge when he suddenly said: 'D'you know, I've got a private bathroom?' "

"Don't be silly."

"Don't be pert, Mrs. Preston," said the judge.

"I'm sorry, my lord, but I don't like the way I'm being questioned," said Anne.

"Very few people do. As a matter of fact I don't like people being questioned in public about their intimate private affairs. But it's the law, so let's get on with it."

"How *did* Mr. Amberley come to tell you that he had a private bathroom?" Coventry continued.

"I think I just knew it. In a hotel one learns or notices these things."

"But you said he told you."

"Well, he may have. All I know is that he had a private bathroom."

"And that his bedroom was on the floor above yours?"

"Yes."

"So that's one way you could have slept with him—he could have come downstairs or you could have gone upstairs?"

"If we'd wanted to."

"Where else could you have made love?"

At this point William Tarrington, Q.C., Coventry's opponent, felt that he should at least give his client some moral support or at any rate breathing space. He also was an able advocate and had been watching Coventry's performance and Anne's struggles with admiration for both. As the judge did not seem prepared to help her, he got up.

"If you had wanted to," he interposed and sat down.

Coventry glared at him.

"That was quite unnecessary," he said. "Of course I meant if she'd wanted to."

"Then you should have said so," said Tarrington from where he sat. Anne looked gratefully at him.

"Would you repeat the question, please?" she said to Coventry and again smiled slightly.

Doubles at tennis, thought Mr. Ringmer. Anne's last words were like a deep lob, giving her time to get back into position. But I mustn't mix my metaphors too much. I've already had music, boxing, road mending, a dog fight and—where does the "upper hand" come from? And now tennis. Anyway, Coventry hasn't a partner, or at any rate she couldn't take part. If Mrs. Amberley suddenly intervened, the judge would soon cut her short. But it was quite a nice idea. Mixed doubles with Anne and Coventry on one side and Mrs. Amberley and Tarrington on the other.

"I asked you where else you could have made love," said Coventry, returning the ball deep into Anne's court. "Where else apart from the hotel?"

"If we'd wanted to," said Anne, "he could have come to my flat, I suppose."

Paragraph eight, thought Mr. Ringer happily. It was like making the witness dig her own grave. How many other counsel could have done it? Making the witness herself give the details of every place where adultery was alleged.

"And did he come to your flat?"

"Once," said Anne. "In the day."

"Why did you say that?"

"Say what?"

"In the day," said Coventry. "Why did you add 'in the day'?"

"Because it was in the day."

"What's that got to do with it?"

"I was just answering your question."

"My question was simply 'did he come to your flat?'" said Coventry. "You said 'once' and then added 'in the day.' Why did you add that?"

"Because it was in daytime."

"Yes, but I didn't ask you what time of day. Why volunteer it?"

"I've no idea," said Anne.

"Haven't you? Isn't it because you thought it sounded better if he came in the day?"

"Possibly."

Down again, thought Mr. Ringmer. Only on one knee perhaps, but she must be feeling a bit groggy already, and the cross-examination had only just started. We're going to win this case. I didn't think all that of the inquiry agent, and Amberley was first class. But it's a true bill and by the time Coventry's finished with Anne there'll only be one possible result. I admire her, though, he thought. She's certainly a fighter. Poor Tarrington never got a chance to knock Mrs. Amberley about. Just a faint suggestion that she'd fallen for the new young manager of her shops. But there wasn't a tittle of evidence against them and Tarrington wasn't entitled to suggest there was anything in it. All he could do was to ask her why she wanted to get rid of such an apparently excellent husband after fifteen years.

"I don't like him," she had said, "and I believe he carried on with other women. When I found he had I started these proceedings."

There was not much Tarrington could do with that. Amberley and Anne's case was that the detective had faked his evidence. But, on the face of it, that was nothing to do with Mrs. Amberley. She gave no incriminating evidence against her husband. And as for her feeling that her husband went with other women, no one could stop her feeling it, if she said she did. Women do feel these things, sometimes with and sometimes without cause, but it doesn't give much scope for cross-examination.

"I didn't say I'd any evidence. I just knew it. A woman knows these things," said Mrs. Amberley. And all Tarrington could say was "If you please," and Mrs. Amberley did please. What a contrast to Coventry's cross-examination of Anne.

"So it's possible you thought it might sound better to say that he came in daytime," he went on. "Why did you want it to sound better if you haven't a guilty conscience?"

"I certainly haven't a guilty conscience."

"Have you a conscience at all?"

"Of course."

"Why? Some people haven't."

"Oh," interposed the judge. "Who?"

Judge Brace would have made an excellent soccer referee. His eye was on the ball and the players the whole time, and, while he never intervened unless it was necessary, he was ready to check counsel if he thought that there was any semblance of unfairness. The question "Have you a conscience at all?" was little more than abuse and could not conceivably help the court to arrive at a just conclusion. Even good advocates occasionally slip in this way and Coventry was quick to realize that he should not have asked the question.

"I accept the rebuke, my lord," he said. "I'm sorry, Mrs. Preston," he added.

"Don't give it another thought," said Anne.

Mr. Ringmer had often wondered how, even in the days of the death penalty, a man charged with murder could laugh out loud at something which happened during his trial. He admired people who could summon up a laugh in times of danger, and he admired Anne for being able to indulge in badinage when she was fighting a desperate fight, not for her life certainly but for something which she appeared to value greatly.

Like the good referee which he was, the judge did not

rebuke Anne for her quip. He would allow a certain amount of unharmful jostling in the hit and thrust of the game. But he would be quick to take action if he thought it was tending to get out of hand.

"So you said 'in the day,' " went on Coventry, "because you wanted it to sound better?"

"I said it," said Anne, "because it was the truth."

"But you also said it because it sounded better."

"If you say so."

"But it's you who said so, Mrs. Preston. Mr. Shorthand Writer, would you very kindly turn up the passage a few questions ago?" The shorthand writer turned back a page of his notebook.

"The Witness," he said, " 'I've no idea.' Counsel: 'Haven't you? Isn't it because you thought it sounded better if he came in the day?' The Witness: 'Possibly.' "

"Thank you," said Coventry.

"You see," said Anne, "I only said 'possibly.' I expect I'll be saying that to all your questions before you've finished with me."

"Will you?" said Coventry. "Have you ever committed adultery with Mr. Amberley?"

"I meant when you'd tired me out," said Anne. "Try again tomorrow afternoon."

"Mrs. Preston," said the judge. "Don't."

"Let's come back to your flat," said Coventry. "If you'd wanted to sleep with Mr. Amberley and he'd come to your flat, day or night would have been all the same to you, wouldn't it?"

"You seem to know all about it."

"Mrs. Preston," said the judge, "this must stop."

"But he's allowed to do it to me."

"Mr. Coventry has a duty to ask you some very unpleasant questions, but he ought not to be deliberately offensive to you. You must not be deliberately offensive to him."

"I'll try, my lord."

"You'd better succeed, Mrs. Preston," said the judge. "Go on, Mr. Coventry."

"If you have a desire for someone and can't see them at night, you'd satisfy it in the day, wouldn't you?"

"As a matter of fact, I *could* see Mr. Amberley at night. In the hotel."

"Thank you."

"Any time," said Anne with a smile.

On this occasion the judge contented himself with giving Anne a warning look, like a referee making a gesture of feeling for his notebook.

"Now tell me, Mrs. Preston," said Coventry, "have you been in Mr. Amberley's car?"

"Yes."

"Has he been in yours?"

"Yes."

"Which is the more comfortable?"

"His."

"Comfortable for what?"

"It was your word, Mr. Coventry."

"In which car would it have been more comfortable to commit adultery?"

"It wouldn't have been comfortable in either."

"How d'you know?"

"Because I have a sufficient imagination."

"Not because you've tried?"

"Not because I've tried."

"But you would have tried if you'd wanted to?"

"I doubt it."

"Why not?"

"Why not? Why not? Why not?" Anne burst out. "Because I don't like the idea. If you want to make love, you want to do it in ample, happy surroundings. Plenty of time, plenty of space—a comfortable bed, a warm thick carpet on the floor . . . Shall I go on?"

"You seem to know all about it."

"Of course I do," said Anne. "I've been married."

"Quite so. And if you'd wanted Mr. Amberley, you'd have liked to have done it properly."

"Of course."

"Either the hotel or the flat would have done nicely for the purpose."

"Yes."

"And the car in an emergency?"

"What emergency?"

"Sudden desire and no other place to go."

"I don't care for the idea."

"But you wouldn't completely rule it out—granted your desire?"

"I can't answer for myself in circumstances which do not exist and never have existed."

"You know why I'm asking these questions, Mrs. Preston, don't you?"

"I've no idea. Because you're paid to do so, I suppose."

"That's just offensive."

"I don't see why. There's nothing to be ashamed of in being paid to do your job."

"Are you not perfectly well aware that there are three specific charges of adultery against you—one in the hotel, one in the flat, and one in the car?"

"Of course I am."

"Then why did you say you couldn't tell why I was asking these questions?"

"Because you run all round the subject," said Anne. "If you'd asked me straight out if I'd committed adultery in any of those places I'd have said—No. No. No."

"But you could have committed adultery with Mr. Amberley in each of those three places if you'd been minded to?"

"Most people in this court could have committed adultery with someone if they'd been minded to."

"Not in those three places."

"Possibly in many more."

"Mr. Coventry," said the judge, "where does that get us?"

"My lord, I first of all want to establish beyond any doubt that these two people had the opportunity to commit adultery in each of the places alleged in the petition."

"Well, you've established that. The question is, did they?"

"I'm coming to that."

"I was wondering when."

"Before I come to the specific allegations, I prefer to cross-examine the witness generally."

"So I see. Tell me when you're coming to the incidents which matter," said the judge.

Mr. Ringmer was now just a shade less happy. The judge was getting bored. If he remained bored, they would lose the case. The petitioner had got to prove that Amberley and Anne had slept together. If there was any real doubt about the proof, the petition would fail. Many cases failed for lack of proof. The mere word of an inquiry agent was seldom sufficient to establish a case against sworn denials. In some actions a judge might become bored because the evidence was so plain that he couldn't understand why so much time was being taken up. That certainly was not so in this case. This case would become plain only if Anne were conclusively shown to be a liar. If Coventry were not able to show that, the result would be that the petition would be dismissed for lack of sufficient certainty. It was boring to be uncertain and if the judge was becoming bored it could only be because he suspected that the truth was not going to emerge. No judge can fail to be interested in the truth. It is his job to try to arrive at it. He knows what a long and difficult journey it may be to reach the goal. He knows that it is sometimes impossible except by luck. But the more difficult it is the more stimulating is the sudden appearance of a sign which seems to point the way. It may be a false one. But when each step follows logically on another and every button pressed reveals a secret nearer to what looks like the truth eventually the answer to the problem stands out clear and certain. Just as in a losing case every point taken on behalf of the losing side, however attractive it seems to be at first, turns out to be bad, so, when a case is going to be established, each signpost points the same way, so that eventually there is only one possible end to the chase. As long as the process of the search for truth is a live one the judge's mind is alert and keen. It is only when the search seems to be leading nowhere that part of the judicial brain sits down on a chair and even puts its feet up and has a nap.

Mr. Ringmer could tell from the judge's remark that

there was a danger that this would happen. Coventry had started off well, unsettling the witness and making her more liable to make a bad impression. But now she appeared to be getting used to Coventry's methods and he had certainly obtained no really valuable answers from her. Well, it was early on and Mr. Ringmer still believed that they would win. If they were going to win, it was because Amberley and Anne had both lied, and, if they had lied, he felt sure that Coventry would in the end establish it. Of course he couldn't do miracles. Mr. Ringmer had lost cases where he had been convinced his client was in the right, but in this present case he sensed that Anne was a liar, that she was putting on a magnificent act but that the truth was in fact as the detective had sworn. But Coventry mustn't bore the judge. He hoped he would change the subject. Coventry's mind had been working on much the same lines.

"Now, Mrs. Preston," he said, "I want to ask you something quite different. Until you went into the witness box I didn't know your name."

"I didn't know yours till I came to court," said Anne.

"The petition refers to you as a woman named Anne."

"Well, I am."

"But no surname."

"Well, you know it now."

"But why did you keep it back?"

"If you were charged with a nasty offense of which you weren't guilty, you might prefer not to give your surname till you had to."

"That would apply equally if I were guilty or not guilty," said Coventry.

"I don't agree. If you're guilty you know you've done it and you've got to take the rap. But if you're innocent and acquitted there will always be some people who'll still think you're guilty. This case might never have come to court. So I kept back my surname as long as I could."

"And that's the only reason we didn't know the name before?"

"Yes."

"But as you stayed at the same hotel as Mr. Amberley we ought to have been able to find your name in the registration book."

"They forgot to ask me to register."

"A curious coincidence that they forgot to ask someone to register and that person doesn't want her name known."

"I didn't mind it being known then."

"But later you did."

"Certainly, to prevent the mud you throw at me sticking. I'll tell you something else. I'd have used a false name for the trial if I could have. But my solicitors wouldn't let me."

"So it was just a bit of luck for you that we couldn't find out your name before?"

"If you like."

"I suggest that it wasn't luck at all, and that you deliberately refrained from registering because you didn't want to be found out."

"I wasn't found out and there was nothing to find out."

"Wasn't there?" said Coventry. "You heard Mr. Brown, the private detective, give evidence yesterday?"

"I did."

"He said, did he not, that on one occasion—on the 19th January, to be exact—he saw Mr. Amberley go into your room?"

"I heard him say that."

"Was that a lie?"

"Probably."

"What d'you mean—probably?"

"What I say," said Anne. "It's probably a lie."

"But why probably? Why not certainly?"

"If you know for certain that it was a lie, I'll take it from you."

"If you say the incident never happened, why do you say it was probably a lie?"

"I didn't say the incident never happened."

"You mean it did happen?"

"Certainly not. The detective said that he saw Mr. Amberley come into my room. Probably he invented it. But it's just possible he made a mistake . . ."

"A mistake? He said it was Room 32 on the first floor."

"Please let me finish. He may have seen Mr. Amberley go into my room when I wasn't there."

"Mr. Amberley had a key then?"

"Certainly not. Many people in this hotel left their doors open. I did anyway. It was the sort of place where *decent* people stayed."

"What was Mr. Amberley going into your room for at all?"

"By mistake, I mean. It was a similar room to his but on a different floor."

"But Mr. Amberley never said in evidence that he went into your room by mistake."

"No one asked him."

"He denied going into your room at all, didn't he?"

"While I was there certainly."

"Surely if he'd gone into it by mistake he'd have said so?"

"I didn't say he did go in, only that he might have. Anyway, if he did go in by mistake he may have forgotten it.

You can't remember all the times you've been into a room by mistake."

"But if he went in by mistake he'd have come straight out again."

"Of course."

"But the detective says he didn't."

"Then he's mistaken or lying."

"How could he be mistaken?"

"How do I know? People do make mistakes, hideous ones sometimes. I don't call people liars unless I have to. But I'm not a barrister."

"Barristers shouldn't call people liars unless *they* have to," said the judge.

"I'm glad to hear it, my lord."

"Tell me, Mrs. Preston," said Coventry, "if you were in the room when the detective says he saw Mr. Amberley go into it he could only have come for one purpose, couldn't he?"

"It might have been for any purpose."

"Are you being serious?"

"Of course I am. How can I tell what purpose Mr. Amberley would have in coming to my room if he never came? He might have wanted to borrow something."

"And stayed for two hours?"

"Why not? He was a friend."

"A little compromising?"

"Certainly if it had happened. But you ask me to say that if he came he must have committed adultery. I don't agree."

"Why should you deny that he came in," said Coventry, "unless you committed adultery?"

"Isn't that a matter for me, Mr. Coventry?" said the judge. "The witness might deny such an episode because she thinks it would go against her. If Mrs. Preston is lying about it, you can say that it's highly suspicious—but it's not conclusive, is it?"

"If your lordship pleases. Mrs. Preston, you say that Mr. Amberley was a friend. How long had you known him?"

"A couple of months."

"Where did you meet?"

"In the bar of the hotel."

"Have you met many people in the bars of hotels?"

"Thousands. Well, hundreds. A good many anyway. But I haven't slept with them."

"I didn't suggest you had—with the exception of Mr. Amberley. I just wondered if it was your normal way of making friends."

"My normal way! Have you never made friends with people as a result of meeting them in the bar of a hotel?"

"Well, I have," said the judge.

"It was pretty much of a pickup, wasn't it?" said Coventry.

"Certainly not, Mr. Coventry," said the judge.

"I'm so sorry, my lord. Mrs. Preston, might we know a little more about you? How would you describe yourself?"

"What do I do?"

"Yes—when you're not making friends with men in the bars of hotels."

"I protest, my lord," interposed Mr. Tarrington.

"So do I, Mr. Coventry," said the judge. "Don't do it again."

"I'm sorry, my lord. I apologize. I just want to know a little about your background, Mrs. Preston."

"I was adopted, if you want to know. D'you want to know why?"

"I'm sorry. I don't want to go as far back as that. Just your way of life for the past—say five years."

"I don't work for a living, if that's what you mean."

"How do you manage to live?"

"My husband left me a little money and I have a widow's pension."

"No regular job?"

"No job at all."

"May I ask what your husband was?"

"He was a bookmaker."

"A bookmaker?"

"Yes, a bookmaker—and he was killed in an air crash. He deliberately crashed into a river to save the lives of children in a field."

"I'm sorry."

"What more would you like to know about me? I had no brothers or sisters and I've no children. I left school at sixteen and went on the stage. In the chorus. Now you're getting somewhere, aren't you? In the chorus, were you? You must have been an attractive little piece. How many men did you sleep with? Well, I'll tell you the answer to that, Mr. Coventry. None. None—till I married my husband. There are girls like that, Mr. Coventry—even if they do make friends with people in the bars of hotels."

"That outburst was quite unnecessary, Mrs. Preston," said the judge.

"It's not so easy to keep calm, my lord, when people sneer at you," replied Anne.

"Mr. Coventry has apologized for that."

"That's easy for him, my lord."

"I'll try not to hurt your feelings, Mrs. Preston," said Coventry. "Tell me, did you like Mr. Amberley?"

"Quite."

"He liked you?"

"I suppose so."

"Did he attract you?"

"Not particularly."

"D'you think you attracted him?"

"I've no idea."

"Did he ever tell you you were attractive?"

"I expect so. Men are always doing that. It doesn't mean a thing."

"You say you never slept with him. If he hadn't been a married man, would you have done so?"

"I've no idea."

"You mean you might have?"

"Of course I might have. We might have got married."

"Do I gather from that answer that you don't approve of extramarital intercourse?"

"What a horrible expression. Do I approve of it between other people, d'you mean?"

"Well?"

"That's their business."

"What about yourself?"

"It would depend on the circumstances."

"So you might have had intercourse with Mr. Amberley if he hadn't been married?"

"I've no idea. If we'd been on a desert island—very likely."

"But you had no physical feeling for him?"

"Certainly not."

"You couldn't have described it as wonderful to be with him?"

"Of course not."

"He was just a man with whom you struck up a mild friendship?"

"Exactly."

"You chatted with him in the hotel where you met; you had one or two drinks together, and once—during the day —he came to your flat in London?"

"Precisely."

"You must have had many similar friendships?"

"A number certainly."

"You've never exchanged love letters with Mr. Amberley?"

"Ridiculous."

"What is his Christian name?"

"You know it as well as I do—Michael."

"Now I want you to look at this piece of paper," said Coventry.

Mr. Ringmer knew what was coming and was not entirely happy about it. He had discussed the matter at length with Coventry and they had both come to the conclusion that it was their duty to use the evidence which was about to be adduced. He himself had nothing whatever to be ashamed of. He was a solicitor of high repute and would never have adopted questionable, let alone illegal, tactics in the conduct of a case. But there was no doubt that such tactics had been used by the inquiry agent, Mr. Brown. The problem which Mr. Ringmer and Coventry had to solve was this: without the slightest suggestion by either of them or, as far as they could tell, from their client, Mr. Brown had obtained most useful evidence by patently improper means. Should they use the evidence so obtained? And if not, why not?

2 Mr. Brown

Mr. Brown, the inquiry agent, was a happy man. He had been a happy boy, a happy youth, a happy young man, and was now happy in his middle age. Although the world is roughly divided into two classes, the happy and the unhappy—those who make the best of every awkward situation and those who make the worst of every situation, even a highly satisfactory one—there are many gradations in each class. Mr. Brown was at the top of the happy class. He had never been sent to prison but, had this happened, he would have accepted his fate philosophically, made friends with prison officers and prisoners, decided how he could put his experience to advantage, and eventually gone out of prison a wiser but no less happy man.

"What a laugh!" he would often say, and this summed up his attitude to life. What a laugh! And, if it was a laugh, it was no good crying over it. At one time he had been a milk roundsman, and a very popular one. He always had a friendly or cheerful word for the customers, even for the unhappy ones who resented cheerful or friendly words. But he did not resent their resentment.

"Top of the morning, my old panjandrum," he would say to the ailing and elderly recluse living at the top of eighty-four steps. "You aren't dead yet, I see. Know how I tell? By the bottles. Leave out six and I'll tell the undertakers. Cheery 'by."

On one occasion he had laughed so heartily at his own brand of humor that he fell down ten of the eighty-four steps and bruised himself badly.

"Not dead yet!" he shouted to the elderly recluse, who was looking somewhat hopefully over the balustrade at Mr. Brown's momentarily still body.

So nearly everyone was sad when Mr. Brown gave up the job. It was his inability from time to time to balance the cash which made his employers regretfully give him notice.

"No hard feelings," he said to his immediate boss when he'd been told the news. "What goes in has got to come out. What a laugh!"

Next he became a window cleaner and everywhere he went he exuded the same good humor. Even when he came at the wrong time or on the wrong day and the householder was not at all pleased to see him.

"Oh dear, oh dear," he would say. "Thursday it is and I've been telling myself all the morning it's Friday. Well, as I'm here, I'd better get on with it, hadn't I? Won't put you out too much? Shan't be a jiffy. No, I won't skimp it, ma'am. Won't leave more smears than I can help."

It was cleaning windows that gave him the idea of becoming an inquiry agent. More than once he had seen things which he was not intended to see and which he had pretended not to see. But it was one special occasion which crystallized the idea which was already starting to form in his mind. He had been innocently cleaning the windows of a house which he thought was on his list when his legs were suddenly pulled from under him and he found himself on the floor of a bedroom with a large man in pajamas standing over him threateningly.

"Oh, no, you don't," said the man. "How much do you weigh?"

Mr. Brown said about nine stone.

"Well, I'm fourteen," said the man. "And they're muscle and bone, not fat. I'll show you."

"I believe you," said Mr. Brown.

"Feeling will make you believe it even more," said the man. He picked Mr. Brown up from the floor, threw him up to the ceiling, caught him just before he hit the ground, threw him up again, caught him again, and then taking him in both hands he shook him very hard indeed. Finally he dropped him on the floor.

"Now," said the man, "we can talk."

Mr. Brown did not look as if he could talk very much but he gave a faint smile of acquiescence.

"Who sent you?"

"The Friston Window Cleaning Company," whispered Mr. Brown.

"Speak up," said the man, "or I'll start on you again."

Mr. Brown repeated what he had said, rather louder.

"Window cleaning company!" said the man in obvious disbelief. "Say that again and I'll throw you *through* the ceiling."

Mr. Brown remained silent.

"Come on," said the man, "who was it?"

It turned out that the big man suspected Mr. Brown of

being employed by a detective agency to watch his movements. Mr. Brown eventually satisfied the man that he really was a window cleaner and not a snooper.

"Well, I'm sorry," said the man. "No bones broken, I hope."

"I hope not," said Mr. Brown.

"That's good," said the man. "But it's hardly my fault if you come to the wrong house, is it?"

"Not your fault at all," said Mr. Brown. "It was entirely mine. I'm sorry to have caused you so much trouble."

"Trouble?" said the big man. "Oh, that! That was nothing, I assure you. Glad you weren't really hurt. But I wanted to make sure you didn't give evidence. And that's as good a way as I know. What do you think?"

"A very good way indeed," said Mr. Brown.

So far from being discouraged by his experience he decided that an inquiry agent's life would be the life for him. Peering into other people's rooms had given him a taste for prying into other people's affairs. He soon got a job with an agency and, after having moved several times from one firm to another, he eventually set up on his own. "The Up-to-Date Detective Agency" he called himself. "Nothing too small, nothing too big. Success almost guaranteed. If he's done it, we'll prove it," he put on his notepaper and in some of his advertisements.

It was the "if he's done it, we'll prove it" that attracted the attention of Mrs. Amberley. She badly wanted a divorce. She had reached the age when a certain type of woman must have her final fling or not at all. And her husband was right in suspecting the new young manager. Mrs. Amberley wanted him very badly. But not just for a night or two. For keeps. And to do that she had to get rid of her husband.

"Mr. Brown," she had said, "I'll pay your normal fees for

whatever you do. But, if you get me a divorce, I'll add £500 to the bill."

Mr. Brown beamed.

"Don't you worry," he said. "You shall have the evidence. My name isn't Brown for nothing." He sometimes used a non sequitur for emphasis.

Later he presented the evidence to Mrs. Amberley and she presented it to her solicitors. The petition was launched and it was about to come on for trial when Mr. Brown produced the additional evidence which had caused Mr. Ringmer's misgivings.

"Let the witness see it, please," said Coventry.

Mr. Ringmer handed a piece of paper to the usher who took it to Anne. She looked at it.

"Where did you get this?" she asked.

"Never mind where we got it," said Coventry. "Read it out, please."

"But I do mind where you got it."

"So you agree it's part of a letter to you?"

"This has been stolen, my lord."

"Not stolen. Borrowed," said Coventry. "You can have it back when the case is over."

Tarrington rose. "My learned friend appears to admit that this note or whatever it is was taken from my client without her authority," he said.

"And, I may say, without mine," added Coventry.

"Then my learned friend agrees," said Tarrington, "that somehow or other my client's property was taken from her unlawfully."

"But not criminally," said Coventry.

"This is as dirty a piece of litigation as I've come across," said Tarrington.

"No dirtier than adultery," said Coventry.

Coventry and Tarrington then proceeded to address the judge in rather louder voices than usual. As they both were speaking at the same time, he could not hear anything either of them said. After the noise had gone on for about a quarter of a minute, he intervened with a loud:

"Shut oop, both of you."

There was an immediate, awed silence.

"Now, Mr. Coventry," the judge went on, "please explain how this piece of paper came into your client's possession."

"Certainly, my lord," said Coventry. "Without my or my client's knowledge a detective managed to obtain entrance into Mrs. Preston's flat and . . ."

"Obtain entrance?" queried the judge. "'Do you mean break in?"

"Yes, my lord."

"Then please say so."

"A detective broke into Mrs. Preston's flat and found this part of a note in the wastepaper basket . . ."

"Not perhaps in the best traditions of English legal procedure," put in the judge.

"I don't pretend it is, my lord. I don't defend the methods."

"You merely seek to use the results?"

"Exactly so, my lord."

"Well, what do you say, Mr. Tarrington?"

"I ask your lordship to refuse to countenance this sort of thing," said Tarrington.

"Of course I don't countenance it. It's disgraceful."

"Then your lordship won't allow the document to be used?"

"I don't know what it is. What is it, Mrs. Preston?"

"It's part of a letter from Mr. Amberley to me," said Anne.

"Then, Mr. Tarrington, how can I rule it out?"

"Because of the way it was obtained. Surely your lordship can say you won't allow a document so obtained to be used for any purpose?"

"Can I? Even in criminal cases I have known police officers obtain evidence unlawfully, but that doesn't prevent it being used as evidence."

"Well, it ought to."

"Then you change the law, Mr. Tarrington."

"But, my lord, in a case of this kind the Court itself would not have ordered my client to produce the document or even to disclose it before the trial. Surely the Court won't allow its own rules to be flouted with impunity?"

"What d'you say to that, Mr. Coventry?"

"Once a witness is in the box and has denied adultery," said Coventry, "I can ask her 'Have you any letters from the respondent?' If she says 'Yes,' your lordship can order her to produce them—even if it meant going home to fetch them."

"The detective has certainly saved her the trouble of doing that," said the judge.

"And, my lord," said Coventry, "I would like to say this in my client, Mrs. Amberley's favor. My client did not know what the inquiry agent was going to do, but even if she had known she might well say—it's all very well for lawyers to have their gentlemanly rules—but I know this woman's committed adultery and if I can get someone into her flat I can prove it. It must be very frustrating to be prevented from doing this."

"Equally frustrating that the police can't bug the house

of every criminal. It is not yet 1984," said the judge.

"My learned friend would like to accelerate our progress there," said Tarrington.

"I resent that."

"Resent it as much as you like."

"Oh, do stop it," said the judge. "No, Mr. Tarrington, much as I disapprove, I don't see how I can rule out the evidence. Of course Mrs. Preston can sue the detective for damages."

"Perhaps Mr. Coventry will appear for me as he disapproves of it so much," said Anne with a slight smile.

"I'm afraid not," said Coventry. "Before you read it out, Mrs. Preston," he went on, "may I assume that, if this piece of paper hadn't been discovered, you would have denied the contents?"

"I expect so," said Anne.

"You agree you would have lied about it?"

"Don't sound so surprised. I tell the truth sometimes."

"Don't be facetious, Mrs. Preston," said the judge.

"If I'd said I'd have admitted it, he'd have suggested I was lying. Wouldn't you?"

"You mustn't ask him questions."

"It's so one-sided."

"It has to be," said the judge. "I shall see that you are not unfairly treated. Go on, Mr. Coventry."

"Now, Mrs. Preston," said Coventry, "would you read out the note. But before you do, is it all in Mr. Amberley's handwriting?"

"What there is of it—yes."

"You know his handwriting well?"

"Well enough."

"You've had other letters from him?"

"One or two. Didn't your agent manage to find them?"

"Perhaps you'd destroyed them."

"What a shame."

"How many were there?"

"I tell you, one or two."

"Did they all begin the same way?"

"No."

"You remember that quite clearly?"

"Not really, but I do remember the first letter I wrote to *him*. Shall I tell you? Or would you like this first?"

"Read that first, please. No—perhaps you'd better tell me what you wrote to him—in case you forget."

" 'Dear Michael,' " said Anne, " 'I think this must be yours. Thanks for a wonderful evening.' Oh, you're quite right. I did use the word wonderful. 'Yours, Anne.' I might have said: 'With love, yours, Anne. P.S. I hope you've got the other.' "

"A glove?"

"Full marks."

"Mrs. Preston," said the judge, "next time I shall fine you for contempt."

"Now, please read out the one in your hand," said Coventry.

"I've thought of another. You wouldn't like that while I still remember?"

"No, thank you. Read it out, please."

" 'Anne, dear, it's only a few minutes since we were together but I feel I must'—oh dear, that's all there is. Couldn't he find another bit?"

"Can you tell me how it went on?"

"I can't think."

"But you can remember your first letter by heart."

"I wrote it. That helps one to remember."

"Have you no idea how this letter of Mr. Amberley's went on? 'You have only just left but I feel I must . . .' Must what?"

"Why didn't you ask him when he was in the box?"

"I may do so later."

"So you were saving it up for me. How flattering. Let me think. Ah, yes—but don't you want him to go out of court while I tell you? Otherwise he can repeat what I say."

"Thank you," said Coventry. "Mr. Tarrington, would you kindly ask your client to go out of court?"

"Certainly," said Tarrington. "Go out of court, please, Mr. Amberley."

Amberley went out.

"Now, Mrs. Preston," continued Coventry, "how did it go on?"

"Words to the effect that he'd enjoyed the evening."

"What had you done together?"

"Had dinner, talked, and what not."

"What not?"

"Not what you mean. We were either in the dining room or the lounge the whole evening."

"Didn't he see you to your car?"

"Certainly. We didn't play hide and seek on the way."

"Did he kiss you good night?"

"I expect so."

"You normally kiss your men friends good night?"

"Usually, if they kiss me."

"Why d'you think he felt he must write to you just after you'd gone?"

"To thank me, I suppose. I believe I'm quite a good talker. And . . ."

"And what?"

"Better still, a good listener. That must have been it. He'd talked to me a lot about his wife. He was very upset about the marriage breaking up. He hadn't wanted it that way. He told me . . . but do you want all this?"

"Go on till I stop you."

"Or me," said the judge.

"He told me that he was very fond of his wife and that he was horrified when she'd told him she didn't love him any more. He said he'd pleaded with her, but with no result. She'd said that either he must leave the house or she would. He couldn't understand it. He couldn't believe there was another man. They'd always seemed so happy. And then suddenly it happened. He was so unhappy. Well, as I say, I'm a good listener, and I suppose I made the right noises at the right times. So he was grateful. And I expect perhaps he was a little bit ashamed of monopolizing the conversation, and wanted to say so."

"You were a comparative stranger," said Coventry. "He called you 'Anne, dear' not 'Dear Anne.'"

"So he did. 'Anne, dear' is more affectionate. He felt affectionate. I'd been kind to him."

"Only by listening?"

"And by being with him when he was lonely and unhappy. And he told me a lot about himself and his wife. D'you want to know?"

"What sort of things?"

"Nothing very spectacular but men love telling their life stories. 'I'm not boring you, am I?' they say and go on before you can stop them. Mind you, I didn't want to stop Michael. He was one of the nicest men I'd met."

"What did he say?"

"He told me about his father who'd been a country par-
son. And then about school. He actually never mentioned
that he'd played fullback for Marlborough until I asked
him. Most men slip it in early—'as a matter of fact,' they
say—"

"Please confine yourself to the facts of this case, Mrs.
Preston," said the judge.

"Well, he said that after he left school he'd rather idled
at Cambridge and then become a schoolmaster. About ten
years later he studied to become a chartered accountant.
That was how he met his wife. Doing her accounts. She was
a very successful businesswoman. With a lot of retail shops.
She became even more successful after they married. And
he adored her. He couldn't think what had happened.
They'd had such a happy partnership both in business and
in bed. Well, I listened to all this. And you must know
yourself it's a help to get things off your chest."

"Let's go back to the letter. The date isn't on it."

"So I see."

"Was it originally?"

"I expect so. Men date letters. It's women who put nothing—or Thursday."

"If it had been dated the 19th January that would have
been written on the date when the detective says he saw
him go into your room."

"Then why should he write me a letter if I'm staying in
the same hotel?"

"There's nothing to show that this was posted. It might
have been a little note slipped under your door. Later that
night."

"It might have said 'Your passionate embraces are better
than anyone else's,' but it didn't."

"D'you swear this letter came through the post?"

"Well, it came through my letter box at my flat, and it had a stamp on. Honestly, I can't remember the postmark."

"Do you swear it wasn't a love letter?"

"Certainly I do."

"Are you a hoarder of letters?"

"No."

"Then why did you keep this one?"

"I didn't, I destroyed it."

"Not until this case was only a few weeks off."

"How d'you know? Oh, of course, that was when your snooper broke in. Have you never kept an unimportant letter longer than it deserved? I'm sorry, I mustn't ask you questions. Well, sometimes I keep letters too long, then I tear them up. Why didn't your snooper bring the other bits he found? There I go again. But I would really like to know."

"The other bits weren't material."

"There might have been other old letters I'd had and torn up about the same time."

"That's perfectly true. I'll have inquiries made."

"Thank you."

"Not at all."

"Do get on. This isn't a tea party," said the judge.

He's getting bored again, thought Mr. Ringmer. But surely the letter must have had some effect. "You've only just gone but I feel I must . . ." Surely the missing words must have been "tell you how much I love you" or something of that sort. Surely the judge could see that. Even a judge who had never wanted to slip a note under someone's door must realize the kind of note it was. "You've only just gone but I feel I must." Well, it would serve them right in a way if the letter didn't make the right impression on the judge, because they ought never to have been able to get hold of it but, on the other hand, having been through the moral struggle on the issue as to whether it was to be used or not and having come to the conclusion that it should be used, it would be very unfortunate if it turned out to be **a** damp squib.

3 Brief Encounter

Coventry had been cross-examining Anne for about half an hour when he realized that something very extraordinary was happening to him. The oddest thing in his career. Possibly the oddest thing in his life. He was falling in love with Anne. It was the words "tea party" that triggered off his appreciation of what had happened. In a flash he could see himself and Anne having tea together on the lawn outside a lovely Georgian house. There was a small stream at the bottom of the garden. He was a happily married family man who would always remain so. He knew that his sudden feelings for Anne were half fantasy and would never be more to him than an outstandingly real dream. But he knew too that it was no dream. How long his cross-examination would go on he did not know, but he knew that while it did there would be passing between him and Anne a flurry of messages, like the arrows from a thousand archers. Normally when a man starts to feel for a woman he wonders whether she feels the same for him and dreads that she does not. But on this occasion Coventry felt sure that it was mutual. A tea party. Buttered scones and a lovely silver teapot poured by Anne. He looked at her. She looked straight back at him. There was no doubt about it. They would only have to be left alone and they would be in each other's arms. Coventry was just thinking how lucky it was for everyone that they never would be left alone when the judge spoke again.

"Well, Mr. Coventry, any other questions?"

"I'm sorry, my lord."

This won't do. I must snap out of it. He knew that this extraordinary love affair, in which the only contact would be by thought and look, would have no effect on his cross-examination. He would question her just as searchingly, just as cruelly, and for just as long as he would have done had she been all the time an ordinary patient on the operating table of the witness box. Counsel cross-examining a witness usually has no more personal interest in the man or woman in the witness box than a surgeon has when he is taking out the gall bladder of a beauty queen. Counsel has to take a professional interest in the nature of the witness, so that he can frame his questions most effectively but beyond noticing if the man has a beard or the woman is attractive he rarely takes any personal interest in the individual whom he is questioning. To Coventry a case was a case and a witness a witness. And, though he would remember the details of an interesting or amusing incident and recount them to his wife or friends later, they made no impact on him. He was able to deal with his practice quite objectively, as do most successful advocates and all happy judges.

"Mr. Coventry," repeated the judge quite loudly.

"Might I have a chair, please, my lord," said Anne, coming to Coventry's rescue, though the judge thought it was emphasizing the delay.

"The witness will need a bed if you don't get a move on, Mr. Coventry," said the judge.

A bed, thought Coventry. No, really, I mustn't.

"Let Mrs. Preston have a chair, usher, please," said the judge. And the chair was brought and Anne sat down.

"Now, Mr. Coventry, please."

"Mrs. Preston—" began Coventry.

"Yes, Mr. Coventry?" said Anne in a softer voice than she had so far used.

"Mrs. Preston," started Coventry again.

"You said that before," grumbled the judge.

"I want to come back to the 19th January," said Coventry.

"Of course," said Anne still softly.

This won't do at all, said Coventry to himself. I've got to smash this woman and, if I go on like this, she'll be smashing me instead. But he couldn't withdraw from their arm's-length embrace without some kind of apology.

"I'm sorry to have to ask you again about the incident," he began.

"Not at all," said Anne. "I understand."

Coventry cleared his throat, a thing he had not done for years when on his feet in court. It is the normal sign of nervousness in an advocate. Many advocates in their earlier days give a slight cough when they get up to cross-examine.

"Thank you," he said.

"All these courtesies are very charming," said the judge, "but they don't help me to decide the case. I wish you'd get on."

This time Coventry did not apologize. Instead he went straight into action.

"You say that on the 19th January Mr. Amberley did not come to your room at the hotel about 9:30 P.M. and stay there for two hours?"

"Certainly not," said Anne. "If he'd stayed for two, he might just as well have stayed the whole night."

"That's what you would have preferred?"

"Certainly, if we'd been having an affair. We'd have done it properly, wouldn't we?"

"Unless one of you was scared of being found out."

"Look, if we'd known we were being followed or watched we wouldn't have done it at all, would we? As it was, he had a room to himself, I had a room to myself. Why shouldn't he stay the whole night?"

"His room might have been found empty in the morning."

"He'd have gone back early in the morning."

"He might have overslept. Had you an alarm clock?"

"Yes."

"Really?"

"But it wasn't working."

"A good reason then for his going early, so that his chambermaid couldn't give evidence of his absence."

"He could have ruffled the bed and pretended he was in the bathroom."

"You forget—he had a private bathroom."

"That's what I mean—he could always say he was in that when the chambermaid came in."

"You seem very skillful at inventing excuses. Have you had much experience of this sort of thing?"

"I'm getting my experience—since I came into the witness box."

"You mean you're simply using your imagination—not drawing on past experiences?"

"I have a very vivid imagination and you manage to spark it off."

"Now let me come to the incident in your flat. That was in February?"

"If you say so."

"Mr. Amberley came to see you. He arrived at twelve noon and left about five P.M."

"No doubt your watcher wrote it down. Still it happens to be true."

"And what happened during those five hours?"

"We talked, we ate, we drank, I believe we slept a bit and—"

"Slept a bit? Where?"

"In the sitting room. In our chairs."

"Not on the sofa?"

"Your snooper should have told you there isn't a sofa. But I have a bedroom, you know."

"You would have used that if you'd been minded to?"

"Of course."

"But you didn't?"

"We didn't."

"Did you want to?"

"I never thought about it."

"He never asked you to?"

"Certainly not."

"What would your reaction have been had he done so?"

"The same as it would be to you."

"Is that true?" said the judge. "You liked Mr. Amberley, you don't like Mr. Coventry."

"I don't mind him, my lord. He's doing his job. I should think he was quite nice out of business hours."

By this time both Coventry and Anne had got back into their pre-tea-party stride. But the statement by the judge that Anne did not like Coventry provoked them both again.

"Yes—quite nice," added Anne.

"Thank you," said Coventry.

"Now, you're not going to start chatting again, I hope," said the judge.

Chatting, thought Coventry. A chat with Anne. I should love it. But this won't do.

"You haven't answered the question, Mrs. Preston," he said. "What would your reaction have been?"

"I did. I said the same as to you—no."

"No?" queried Coventry.

"I'm afraid so," said Anne with a slight smile.

"So after you'd eaten, drunk, and slept," went on Coventry, "he went home?"

"He went away. He had no home. His wife had seen to that."

"You seem to feel very protective toward Mr. Amberley?"

"I feel sorry for him, very sorry. Turned out of his house for no reason and then brought here for no reason either."

"Of course, you've only heard his side of the case."

"I heard what she said in court. Even here she said nothing whatever to justify turning him out of his house. A man who's had a home for twenty years to have to go and live in a hotel."

"A hotel has certain advantages."

"Don't, Mr. Coventry," said the judge.

"My lord?"

"Don't appear too dense, Mr. Coventry. If you simply mean that everything's done for you in a hotel, the remark is wholly irrelevant to this case. If you were implying that at a hotel you meet people—people with whom you could commit adultery and have the opportunity to do so, it was an unpleasant and unfair comment."

"I'm sorry, my lord."

"So I should think. Now, let's get on."

Tarrington got up. "It isn't the first time my learned friend has done this sort of thing," he said, "but I thought it best not to intervene."

"Pity you didn't think it best this time," said the judge.

"But, my lord, you've just said—"

"Exactly. So why should you?"

Tarrington sat down.

"Now, I'm sorry to have to ask you these next questions, Mrs. Preston," said Coventry, "but I'm afraid I must. You've been a widow for five years? I imagine that you're a normal woman with normal sexual instincts."

"Yes."

"Have you never wanted a man in that five years?"

"Certainly."

"But never had one?"

"Have I got to answer these insulting questions about the whole of my private life, my lord?"

"I think you'd better," said the judge.

"Then the answer is no."

"But if the opportunity had coincided with the desire you would have satisfied it?"

"Possibly. If I'd been asked."

"You liked Mr. Amberley."

"I've already said so."

"You've kissed him, he's kissed you?"

"Only once I told you. A good-by kiss."

"Never anything more?"

"Never."

"You're quite sure of that?"

"Quite."

"That's as true as the rest of your evidence?"

"Oh dear! I thought that that question went out fifty years ago," said the judge.

"It's a legitimate question," said Coventry.

"But what good does it do? Some witnesses may tell the truth on the vital matters but tell one lie on something less important and stick to it. Then you say to them 'is that answer as true as the rest of your evidence?' Of course, they'll say it is. What else can they say? And then you ask me to disbelieve the whole of their evidence because they've admitted that it is on a par with the one untruthful answer. Well, you can ask as much as you like."

"You haven't heard the witness's answer yet, my lord," said Coventry.

"What do you expect her to say?" replied the judge. "That her answer was more truthful or less truthful than the rest of her evidence? Witnesses are human beings, you know. And so are judges."

"I'm sorry to have displeased you, my lord."

"You don't mind in the least."

"Mrs. Preston," said Coventry, breaking off from his argument with the judge, "you said you'd only kissed and been kissed by Mr. Amberley in a good-by context. Is this true?"

"It is."

"You also said that you've never been to bed with Mr. Amberley. Is that true?"

"It is."

"Is the one answer as true as the other?"

"Yes."

"Or as false?"

"I don't understand what you mean."

"You see, Mr. Coventry," said the judge, "where is it getting you?"

"The witness is evading the issue," said Coventry.

"The witness is doing nothing of the sort. She merely refuses to be drawn. And in my view quite rightly. It's a footling question anyway."

"I beg your lordship's pardon?"

"I said it was a footling question," repeated the judge.

"I respectfully protest."

"You protest away—but don't say respectfully. You don't mean it. Now, have you finished your cross-examination?"

"Nothing like, my lord. But before I go on with it I want to make an application to your lordship. It's rather unusual, I'm afraid."

"What is it, Mr. Coventry?"

"I want permission to ask Mr. Amberley another question now."

"Why won't it wait? He can be recalled later."

"I should prefer to ask it now."

"So you say, but why?"

"I don't think it would be in the interests of justice to tell your lordship at this stage."

"So you won't tell me the grounds for your application?"

"I'd rather not."

"That's a new one on me."

"I said it was unusual."

"That's an understatement. What do you say, Mr. Tarrington?"

"My lord, I most strongly object," said Tarrington.

"Why?"

"I've never heard of such an application."

"Well, you have now," said the judge. "What harm will it do you?"

"Well, my lord—it will—my lord—it will—"

"Come along, Mr. Tarrington, what harm will it do?"

"I don't know what the object is."

"Nor do I and neither of us will unless I grant the application. Very well, Mr. Coventry, let Mr. Amberley be recalled."

"Call Mr. Amberley, please," said Tarrington. "And I suppose my learned friend would like Mrs. Preston out of court while he gives evidence."

4 The Worrier

What was Coventry up to? thought Tarrington. William Tarrington was a rare type at the bar. He was a successful worrier. Very occasionally a Lord Chancellor makes a mistake and recommends the appointment to the bench of a barrister because of his generally acknowledged success, without appreciating that the successful man is a worried man too. Such appointments are always a failure. The only successful judge of that kind died from worry within a couple of years of his appointment. So it is not really kind or true to describe him as a successful judge. It is not much good being the most excellent judge if you don't live to judge for a number of years. The Lord Chancellor must take a chance on accident or illness removing a judge prematurely, but he should not knowingly take a chance with a worrier. The worrier judge is either a bad judge or, if he is a good one, he dies too soon.

At the bar it doesn't matter except to the man himself and his family and friends. And the work has nothing to do with it. If you worry you will worry just as much if you are a plumber and when on holiday on Margate beach worry whether your repair of a particular high-pressure water pipe will hold, or whether you are a surgeon and wonder whether your patient's unexpected deterioration is due to a swab left inside him or your bad handling of the operation or just to nature's way. You will worry on the way to work, during the lunch hour, and on the way home. And often you will worry yourself to sleep. If your worrying nature is of too high a degree you will commit suicide. Fortunately this extreme of worry is rare. At the other end of the scale there is the person who worries a bit but not too much or too often, and between him and the suicidal type there is an infinite variety of the breed. Whether the tendency to worry is hereditary or acquired or a bit of both there is nothing that can be done about it. You have to learn to live with it, and most worriers can lead reasonably happy lives. The busier lives they lead the less time they can have to worry. You cannot work and worry at the same time. You cannot consciously enjoy yourself and worry at the same time. It is in the interval between work and play or work and work or play and play that the worrier has his unhappy moments. So the advice to give to a worrier is to do as much as possible by way of work or play. You cannot seriously listen to a Beethoven symphony and worry whether Mrs. Jones recognized you at the hairdresser's. You'd hate to appear to cut Mrs. Jones but it's difficult to tell whether she's actually looking at you. You hadn't the time to go right up to her and say something. So you gave a feeble sort of grin and left hurriedly. But shouldn't you have made the time? It would have taken only a few seconds. And then there'd have been no doubt about it. But she is rather a talker and might have kept you. And it's difficult to drag yourself away from her without appearing rude. And Mrs. Jones is rather inclined to say of people, "Oh—she hasn't much time for me, I'm afraid. I've nothing to offer." Would it have been better to risk the delay and avoid the worry afterwards? Well, if you are a worrier and seriously dislike hurting people's feelings, you can go on like this for a long time. And it will be quite a test for Beethoven whether he or Mrs. Jones wins, because, of course, you can let the music go on while you worry over Mrs. Jones but you won't hear a note of it. People who say that they can read a book and *listen* to music at the same time are unaware of the truth that, unless you happen to be one in a million, you cannot. Except for the handful of people in the world who can write a letter and dictate another at the same time, it is physically impossible to concentrate on two things at once.

Tarrington could be described as an upper-middle-class worrier. As a young man at the bar he had suffered torments of worry. Justice among human beings not being perfect, it has to be admitted that young Tarrington in his early days lost cases which he ought to have won. Later he won cases which he ought to have lost. It is to be feared that he did not worry overmuch about those. He obeyed the rules of advocacy and if, without any impropriety, he could win a doubtful case, so much the better. But when he lost a case which he ought to have won, and on the way back from court he suddenly realized the question he ought to have asked (or ought not to have asked), or the answer to the judge's question which he ought to have made and did not make, or when on returning to chambers he turned up a law report and saw that he had a complete answer to his opponent's submissions, then in any of the cases—and they all happened—his anguish was great.

As he became more experienced and more skillful he made fewer and fewer mistakes and began to have much greater confidence in his own judgment, but there was still plenty to worry about. He did not worry while he was actually conducting the case. He had no time to do so. It was in the intervals. In the Amberley case he very much wanted to know what the truth was. He had seen both his clients in conference, both separately and together. Both of them had strenuously denied the charges against them. But with a difference. There was a quiet confidence about Amberley which strongly suggested that the man was speaking the truth. But, although Anne was much more bitter in her denunciation of the petitioner, Mrs. Amberley, Tarrington had the feeling, when he questioned her, that she might be putting on an act. He was quite used to guilty people denying their guilt with the utmost tenacity. The mere fact that a client of his denied something alleged against him did not make him either believe or disbelieve the denial. For one thing, except to the extent to which it affected his conduct of the case, he was not concerned with the truth or untruth of his client's statement. It was his duty to put forward his client's case for better or for worse and whether he believed in it or not. Of course in some cases his disbelief in his client's story might lead him to advise a settlement of the matter. But you can't settle divorce cases, certainly not cases of the Amberley kind. What troubled Tarrington in his worrying moments was his belief in Amberley and his curious distrust of Anne. But, if Anne was lying, then Amberley must be too. Yet, if Amberley was telling the truth, why did he have this feeling about Anne? If he was telling the truth, she must be telling it too. It did not affect his conduct of the case, but he had never had a similar experience and, as worry was part of his makeup, he worried about it when he had the opportunity.

Presumably Coventry expected to get a statement from Amberley which was contrary to Anne's evidence. Perhaps he had deliberately not asked Amberley before in order to get a statement from Anne which Amberley would have to deny. But if Amberley was telling the truth, why should there be a discrepancy between them on an important matter? On trivial matters one would expect there to be discrepancies. Indeed few truthful witnesses would give exactly the same account of an occurrence. It is sometimes a pointer toward false evidence that the witnesses say the same thing almost parrot-wise. But this must be something important. An advocate of Coventry's ability would not dream of emphasizing the point as he had done by his unusual application unless, first, it was a matter of substance and, secondly, he was likely to succeed on it. It would be a considerable bathos and harm Coventry's case if nothing came of his maneuver. Well, he would soon know. Amberley was already in the witness box.

"You're still on oath, Mr. Amberley," said the judge.

"I understand, my lord."

Then Coventry began.

"Mr. Amberley," he said, "previously you gave evidence that you'd never committed adultery with Mrs. Preston. That was true?"

"Certainly."

"Had you wanted to?"

"I suppose I had as a matter of fact."

"Why didn't you?"

"Because I'm married."

"You disapprove of adultery then?"

"I don't think I'd commit it myself."

"You don't *think*."

"I can't answer for what I'd do in all possible circumstances at all possible times. If, as I hope, I win this case but my wife refuses to live with me, I cannot guarantee that never at any time will I commit adultery. I hope not but I can't be sure."

"You say you didn't sleep with Mrs. Preston but you'd have liked to. Did you kiss her?"

There was a pause. "Did you kiss her?" Coventry repeated.

"Yes—once—no, twice."

"Good-by kisses?"

"More than that."

"You said you kissed her when you weren't saying good-by?"

"Yes."

"When?"

"Once was at her flat."

"How long did that take?"

"How long? Oh, I see. Oh—a minute or so."

"You didn't have an egg timer with you?" put in the judge.

"No, my lord."

"About the same time on each occasion?"

"About."

"What sort of kisses were they? Passionate?"

"Moderately so."

"Were they just kisses? Nothing else?"

"No, nothing else. They were the sort of kisses a man might exchange with a girl when they liked each other but had no intention of carrying the matter further."

"Anyway they were not good-night pecks."

"No."

"And where were they exchanged?"

"Once in Mrs. Preston's flat and once in my car."

"How did they come about? The flat first."

"We were standing by the fireplace. I drew her toward me and kissed her. She didn't object. So I kept on for a bit."

"Did she respond?"

"Yes, but not immoderately."

"She took her cue from you?"

"If you like to put it that way."

"Why didn't you persist to see how far she'd go? You'd have liked to?"

"Purely physically I would have liked to, but I tell you I had no intention of committing adultery."

"What about the occasion in the car? Was that before or after the occasion in the flat?"

"After."

"How did that come about?" asked Coventry.

"I was driving her home. I said, 'If I stopped the car and kissed you, would you mind?' "

"What did she say?"

"Try it and see."

"So you tried it?"

"Yes."

"And what did you see?"

"How d'you mean? It was dark in the car. I couldn't see anything."

"And that went on for a minute or so?"

"About."

"And then what happened?"

"I said, 'I suppose we'd better go on.' "

"And she said?"

" 'I suppose so.' "

"Did she seem reluctant to stop the kissing?"

"I think so but of course I can't know that she felt the same as I did. There was no point in going on. It could lead nowhere."

"But it was nice while it lasted."

"I presume so."

"Don't you *know?*"

"I didn't analyze my feelings at the time; I kissed her because I wanted to. So presumably I enjoyed it. But I can't pretend it was entirely satisfying."

"You'd have liked it to go further?"

"I've told you. From the purely physical point of view, yes."

"That is all I wish to ask," said Coventry.

Tarrington no longer wondered what Coventry was up to.

5   The Two Kisses

Mr. Ringmer was very pleased indeed. How artistically Coventry had done it. He had wondered why Coventry had not asked Amberley questions of this kind when he had first cross-examined him. But now he knew. Coventry had realized that these two were not easy to catch. If Amberley had given evidence about the kisses before Anne gave evidence, she would have admitted them. Coventry had waited for her denials before he questioned Amberley on the subject. He had taken the small risk that the judge would not permit the recall of Amberley, but it was most improbable that this would not be allowed at some stage, and it was a chance well worth taking.

But why should Amberley tell the truth about the matter and Anne lie? That was certainly odd. And now what would she do? Continue to deny the kisses? But how could she? There could be no mistake about the matter. No one could confuse the good-by pecks to which she had referred with the kisses spoken of by Amberley. She could hardly say that Amberley was a liar. But she had the choice of saying that or admitting that she had lied. Quite plainly the judge would not believe her if she said that Amberley was wrong. What possible reason could he have for making such an admission if it was not true? That was clear enough. But why had Anne lied? If she had had a lower intelligence, there would not have been much of a problem. Stupid people who have no particular morals may lie against their own interests. But not people of Anne's type. Well, the first question was which evil would she consider the lesser, to admit to lying or to call Amberley a liar? And then if she chose what seemed probably the better course, what excuse would she give for the lie?

A few moments later Anne was summoned back to the witness box and Coventry opened the attack.

"Mrs. Preston," he said, "I want to ask you again. Do you say that you have never kissed Mr. Amberley other than good-by?"

"No."

"What do you mean, no?" asked Coventry. "Are you agreeing with me?"

"I seldom do," said Anne, again with the suspicion of a smile. "But what am I supposed to be agreeing with?"

"You swore earlier and quite positively that you had never kissed him except when you said good-by. Was that true?"

"Not really, no."

"You admit you lied?"

"I suppose I did."

"Why?"

"Because it's all so unfair."

"What's unfair?"

"The whole of these proceedings. A wretched husband is turned out of his home for no reason at all, he makes friends with me, snoopers break into my flat, lie about our being in the same bedroom together, and then I'm cross-examined as though I were a prostitute. All right, we did kiss each other. Twice. Once in my flat and once in the car. But that was all."

"But you never committed adultery?"

"Certainly not."

"But you were just as positive when you said you hadn't kissed."

"Kissing is quite a different thing."

"No doubt it is, Mrs. Preston, but if you lie about the one, how is the judge to know that you are not lying about the other?"

"How is he to know that I am? Because I lied over a trivial thing, that doesn't mean I'd lie over an important one."

"Why do you now admit that you lied about the kissing?"

"I'd have thought that was obvious. I realize that you must have asked Mr. Amberley and I know that he wouldn't lie about anything. He's a good man, much too good for his wife. It's not fair the way you're getting at him through me."

"But what was the point of denying that you'd kissed?" asked the judge.

"I thought Mr. Coventry would make too much of it. If you kiss, why do you kiss? If you have an urge, why don't you satisfy it? And so on. I could hear the questions before he asked them. I thought it simpler to avoid them. I'm sorry, my lord. It was silly of me."

"It was perjury," said Coventry.

"Was that a question or a comment?" said the judge.

"I'm sorry, my lord."

"Isn't it a sign of honesty on Mrs. Preston's part to make the admission?" the judge went on.

"It's the first time I've heard an admission of perjury called a sign of honesty, my lord."

"There has to be a first time, Mr. Coventry," said the judge.

Well, thought Mr. Ringmer, she took the right course from her point of view and has got away with it as well as she could. A pity. But why did she take the risk in the first instance? If she and Amberley were guilty, as they surely were, they must have talked about the case before it came on and decided what to say. The kissing episodes were obvious matters to discuss. Should they admit or deny them? Of course, if they were innocent, there was no need to discuss them, but why then should Anne deny that they had happened? Mr. Ringmer regretfully came to the conclusion that Anne's explanation might be the true one. Innocent people fighting a case do sometimes lie to try to improve their prospects of acquittal. It is a silly thing to do but it happens. Anne, though intelligent, might be a liar by nature. And just as some people who defraud the customs authorities think that everyone else does the same, so Anne might conceivably have assumed that Amberley would lie about the kisses. After all, no one saw them kiss on those occasions. Why make a present of them to the other side unnecessarily? Yes, thought Mr. Ringmer, we haven't won the case by a long way yet. Coventry has still a lot of work to do.

6 The Diary

While Coventry was continuing to cross-examine Anne Mr. Ringmer was told by his clerk that Mr. Brown wanted to see him urgently. He left the Court and met Mr. Brown in the corridor.

"I've got some more dope for you," said Mr. Brown. "It took my breath away. This'll do the trick if nothing else does."

"What is it?" said Mr. Ringmer.

"It cost £50," said Mr. Brown.

"Never mind that," said Mr. Ringmer, who knew that within reason his client would pay anything to get her divorce. "What is it?"

"It'll split your sides," said Mr. Brown.

"Never mind my sides," said Mr. Ringmer, "what's the information?"

"It'll kill you," said Mr. Brown.

"Mr. Brown," said Mr. Ringmer a little testily, "kindly tell me what you have to say. I want to get back to court."

"It's as good as over," said Mr. Brown.

"It is very far from as good as over," said Mr. Ringmer. "What information have you got?"

"Well," said Mr. Brown, "you know I saw them canoodling in the back of a car."

"Canoodling?" repeated Mr. Ringmer.

"It's a nicer word," said Mr. Brown.

"Well?"

"Well," said Mr. Brown, "it isn't the first time."

"What isn't the first time?"

"It's not the first time she's canoodled in the back of a car."

"Another divorce case?"

"No," said Mr. Brown, "but as good as."

"Please come to the point."

"Magistrate's Court. Charge of indecency with a man in the back of a car."

Mr. Ringmer became keenly interested.

"How long ago?"

"Haven't got the date."

"Then haven't you a record of the conviction?"

"I didn't say she was convicted," said Mr. Brown.

"What!" said Mr. Ringmer.

"It's a pity," said Mr. Brown. "No, she wasn't actually convicted. That would have been too good to be true. But this is almost as good as."

"Given an absolute discharge, I suppose?" suggested Mr. Ringmer.

"She was discharged, all right," said Mr. Brown.

"But did the bench find the charge proved?"

"Well, no," said Mr. Brown. "They didn't go as far as that."

"Was she acquitted then?"

"As a matter of fact," said Mr. Brown, "she was."

"What the hell's the good of that?" said Mr. Ringmer angrily. He did not usually employ such language but he was really annoyed.

"I thought you'd be pleased," said Mr. Brown.

"Pleased!" repeated Mr. Ringmer. "What is there to be pleased about?"

"Well, look, sir," said Mr. Brown, "I walked up to the back of the car and what did I see?"

Mr. Ringmer said nothing.

"Come on, sir, what did I see?" Mr. Brown persisted.

"You say you saw them—er—at it," said Mr. Ringmer.

"Right," said Mr. Brown, "but they say I'm a liar or mistaken."

"Well?"

"Well, sir, of course I'm telling the truth and I'm not mistaken, but for the sake of argument, sir, let's pretend I am a liar or am mistaken."

"Well?" said Mr. Ringmer impatiently.

"Well, sir," went on Mr. Brown, "three years ago or whenever it was a policeman said he saw her at it in the back of a car. Now the bench said *he* was a liar or mistaken. But they didn't know what was going to happen three years later. And the judge here doesn't know what happened a few years ago—yet. But who's going to believe that twice on different occasions two different people have looked into the back of a car and seen the same woman doing precisely nothing? We can't both be wrong."

Mr. Ringmer thought for a moment, and his anger lessened.

"You're saying that, even though she was acquitted, it's

a very odd coincidence that different men should lie or be mistaken about her movements in the back of a car."

"I am saying that very thing, sir," said Mr. Brown.

"I'll have a word with Mr. Coventry as soon as I can," said Mr. Ringmer. "Stay here, please."

Mr. Ringmer went into court. He waited patiently until he thought he could say a quick word to Coventry. The experienced solicitor knows that it is a dangerous thing to interrupt counsel in the middle of a speech or cross-examination, not simply because he risks a snub—that is an occupational hazard—but because he takes counsel's mind off the particular point with which he is dealing.

There are counsel who refuse to be interrupted in the middle in any circumstances. It is related that on one occasion an eminent silk of this kind was in the middle of a lengthy cross-examination when his solicitor, who had been summoned out of court much as Mr. Ringmer had been, came back into court in a state of great excitement and tried to speak to his counsel. At first he was just ignored. When counsel found that the solicitor persisted, he hissed at him: "Please wait." The solicitor disregarded the request. "Be quiet, will you," said counsel angrily, more like a schoolmaster talking to a boy than a barrister addressing his client. Even this did not check the solicitor. Eventually the eminent silk was compelled to give way.

"Forgive me, my lord," he said to the judge, plainly indicating that he needed a moment to brush off this irritating fly of a solicitor who was tickling him. He then addressed the solicitor.

"Well, what is it?" he said angrily, and added with heavy sarcasm, "I suppose the client's dead."

"Yes," said the solicitor.

Fortunately for Mr. Ringmer Coventry was not like that particular silk. Moreover, he knew the difference between his professional clients, and in particular he knew that Mr. Ringmer was not a man to interrupt except for a good cause.

"Forgive me, my lord," he said when he realized that Mr. Ringmer was trying to attract his attention, "might I have a word with my client?"

"Certainly, Mr. Coventry."

"I'm most grateful, my lord."

Mr. Ringmer then asked Coventry if he could get an adjournment for two or three minutes. He did not know for how long Coventry would go on cross-examining Anne, but, more important than that, he wanted Coventry to be able to use this new material at the most appropriate time. That was a matter only Coventry could judge.

"It's not very convenient," said the judge. "My room is miles away from here."

"I'm so very sorry, my lord," said Coventry, "but I'm told the matter is important."

"Very well," said the judge. "I'll give you five minutes."

"I'm most grateful to your lordship," said Coventry.

"I won't rise," said the judge. "That'll keep you to your five minutes."

Coventry left the Court followed by Mr. Ringmer. Mr. Brown was waiting in the passage.

Mr. Ringmer began to explain.

"Would you like to speak to the witness?" he asked Coventry when he had told him the source of his information.

"No, I think not," said Coventry. Counsel only interview witnesses (other than their clients and expert witnesses) on special occasions. This did not appear to Coventry to be such an occasion.

"Which court was it?" asked Coventry.

"He doesn't know. Apparently he paid a man £50 for the information."

"Who's the man?"

"He didn't say," said Mr. Ringmer.

"You'd better ask him," said Coventry, "and at the same time find out how the man knew about it."

Mr. Ringmer went over to Mr. Brown and put Coventry's questions to him.

"Now, this is going to surprise you," said Mr. Brown.

"What was your informant's name?" repeated Mr. Ringmer.

"Hold tight," said Mr. Brown.

Mr. Ringmer said nothing.

"It wasn't me," said Mr. Brown. "I tell you I paid £50 for it."

"Will you kindly tell us the man's name," said Mr. Ringmer. "We've very little time."

"It'll give you a shock," said Mr. Brown. "I should stand nearer the wall, if I were you."

"Mr. Brown," said Mr. Ringmer, "the judge has given us exactly five minutes. You've wasted three of them already."

"Brown," said Mr. Brown.

"His name was Brown? The same as yours?"

"I told you it'd shake you. But it's true as I'm standing here. And another thing. He's an inquiry agent too. That's how he knew."

"But how did you get hold of him?" asked Mr. Ringmer.

"Where I get most of my information," said Mr. Brown. "In a boozer."

"It was a pure coincidence?"

"Put it that way if you like."

"But how d'you know he's talking of the same person?"

"He saw her picture in the paper. That's how he came to tell me. 'I've seen that face afore,' he says. So, of course, I asked him when. 'Three years ago,' he says. 'Where?' I asks. 'At Brinstead police court,' he says. 'No, I'm a liar,' he says, 'that was another case. But it was in a police court anyway.' And then he told me all about it."

Mr. Ringmer conveyed this information accurately to Coventry, who thought for a moment or two.

"A bit indefinite," he said. "I shall have to feel my way cautiously, in case it's the wrong person. And, even if it's a true bill, Tarrington will raise hell when he knows she was acquitted. The judge may too. But, all the same, if it did happen, it's almost unbelievable that it could happen again to the same person. Very well, then, we'll go back and I'll wait for the right moment. I think I'll deal with the diary next."

They went back into court. The judge looked at his watch.

"You've just done it, Mr. Coventry," he said.

"Glad not to have kept your lordship waiting," said Coventry.

"But I've been waiting for five minutes," said the judge.

"Very good of your lordship," said Coventry. "Now, Mrs. Preston, I'd like you to look at this diary. Hand it to the witness, please, usher."

Mr. Ringmer handed a diary to the usher who took it to Anne.

"Is that your diary, madam?" asked Coventry.

"Yes, it is," said Anne, "where did you get it? Oh, of course it was stolen with the letter."

"Not stolen, madam. You can have it back after this case is over."

"I really must protest, my lord," said Tarrington. "I cannot think of strong enough language to use to describe my feelings."

"Good," said the judge. "But your feelings don't matter. You'd better address yourself to mine. Do you object to the introduction of the diary as evidence?"

"Most certainly."

"Isn't it in the same position as the letter?"

"Yes, my lord."

"Well, I've allowed that in, how can I keep this out?"

"It's a matter of discretion, my lord."

"But is it? If it were, I might very well refuse to allow the petitioner to have the benefit of this sort of evidence. Unlike you, I can find language to describe it. It's quite deplorable."

"My lord, if I may say so," put in Coventry, "I respectfully agree and might I add that no English lawyer of repute would be a party to it?"

"You and your solicitor are of the highest repute, if I may say so," said the judge.

"Thank you, my lord," said Coventry.

"I should wait before you thank me. Being of such good repute, how comes it that you are prepared to use a document which is obtained in such deplorable circumstances? You wouldn't do it yourselves but you're quite prepared to take advantage of it if someone else does the dirty work."

"We considered this point most carefully, my lord," replied Coventry. "I came to the conclusion that we either must retire from the case or use the evidence. If the petitioner herself had been a party to the outrage—and I do not mince my words, my lord—if she had been a party to it, my solicitor and I would probably have refused to act for her any longer. But she assures us that it was entirely the inquiry agent's doing. That being so, the evidence is available and, in my view, we have a duty to our client to continue to represent her and to put in the evidence."

"I entirely disagree with my learned friend," said Tarrington.

"Well, what would you have done, Mr. Tarrington?"

"What would I have done?"

"Yes."

"I'd have to think about that, my lord."

"Well, your learned opponent has thought about it. If his client is innocent in the matter, and if the evidence is here, why mustn't he put it in?"

"Well," said Tarrington for want of a better answer, "I ask you to refuse to allow him."

"I know, but you don't tell me what power I have to refuse." The judge turned to Anne. "Mrs. Preston, is that your diary?"

"Yes."

"Very well, Mr. Coventry, ask your next question."

"Will you be good enough to turn up the entry for the 19th of January?" said Coventry.

Anne turned over the page.

"Yes, I have it," she said.

"What does it say?"

"You want me to read it out loud?"

"Yes, please."

"It's private. My own private thoughts."

"What were they on the 19th of January?"

"This is disgraceful, my lord," said Anne.

"It is a bit," said the judge, "but I'm afraid you must do what you are asked."

"To read it out?"

"Yes, please. Every word."

"It just says 'Michael. A wonderful night.'"

"And was it, Mrs. Preston?" asked Coventry.

7 The Judge's Mind

Judge Brace was not happy about the case. It was the first defended petition he had tried, though he had had considerable experience of divorce cases when at the bar. County Court judges in London do not ordinarily try defended divorce cases, though they do occasionally. It is the undefended cases that are normally handed over to them for better or for worse. But opinions vary considerably as to what is better and what is worse. Some people think that the important thing is that married couples who don't get on should be able to get divorces without delay or fuss. Others think that until Parliament alters the law (which does not allow divorces simply by consent and insists that a genuine matrimonial offense should have been committed before a decree can be granted) the judges should observe it. There is much to be said for both points of view. Apart from religious considerations, it cannot be desirable that men and women should be compelled to remain married if it is clear that they cannot get on. If there are no children, there seems little reason for binding them together, provided they have really tried to make a success of their marriage and failed. If there are children, it must be arguable whether it is better for them to be brought up in an atmosphere of friction and hostility or for them to go from one parent to another and back again. Neither solution is a good one, and which is the better must depend on the circumstances of each case. So divorces should be granted if it is for the benefit of the children. The other point of view is that it brings the law into contempt if it is virtually ignored and decrees of divorce granted freely, when it is fairly obvious that the parties have arranged the case between them.

Judge Brace was a common-sense judge and on the whole he steered a middle course. If a case appeared obviously collusive, he would not let it through. But he did not look for trouble. So, on the whole, practitioners liked to appear before him in undefended cases.

It was as well for them that he took the course which he did. He had a very astute mind and could in many cases have nosed out collusion or connivance had he been minded to do so. He was a keen reader of detective stories and, so long as the problem was fairly told, he nearly always reached the correct solution. Logic was his stand-by. His theory was that, by the time you came to the end of a case, there must be no inconsistencies, and he rarely arrived at a decision which did not satisfy the logical test.

The difficulty with which the judge was faced in the Amberley case was this: the main evidence against the husband and Anne was given by the inquiry agent. The judge was not at all impressed by this evidence. He knew inquiry agents of old and that they were perfectly capable of faking a case entirely if they couldn't get the evidence which they wanted. Mr. Brown was certainly not at all outstanding as a witness. His evidence was definite enough but might be completely untrue. Amberley, on the other hand, had given his evidence excellently and with conviction. He had made a very good impression on the judge, and, as between him and Mr. Brown, the judge would not have had the least hesitation in rejecting the inquiry agent's evidence and accepting the husband's. Anne's evidence, however, was quite a different matter. The judge as a man could not help being fascinated by the beauty and determination of the woman, but as a judge he felt that she was a particularly unreliable witness. But it seemed inescapable that, if she was lying about her relationship with Amberley, so was he. Here was an inconsistency which puzzled him greatly. Coventry and Mr. Ringmer read the judge's mind rightly when they said to themselves that to win the case it was essential that Anne should be destroyed as a witness.

The judge had watched Anne most carefully from the moment she had come into the witness box. Much more than usual he had not only noted the inflections of her voice but the expressions on her face. Of course, he could not stare at her the whole time, and he must have missed some of her facial reactions to questions, but he looked at her as often as he could without its leading to embarrassment. By the time the diary episode had been reached the judge was very far from satisfied that she was a reliable witness. It was true that she had emerged from her lie about the kisses more unscathed than might have been expected. Her explanation of her lie might be true, and her explanation of her admission probably was true. But the episode certainly did nothing to improve the effect of her evidence as a whole. But the diary episode was unsatisfactory from any point of view. It would have revolted most people to learn that evidence had been obtained in such a scandalous manner. This fact alone would have made most judges hope that the petitioner would not gain much from evidence so obtained. But if there were admissions in the diary they must be given due weight. But—and here was the real puzzle—if she had slept with Amberley, Amberley had slept with her. Listening to Amberley, the judge thought he was innocent. Listening so far to Anne, he suspected that she was guilty. But one could not be innocent and the other guilty in fact. Of course the laws of evidence sometimes produced this very odd-sounding result. For example, if a wife confessed adultery to her husband and there was no other evidence of adultery, the husband could get a decree of divorce against his wife, if the Court believed the confession to be genuine, although his case against the corespondent would fail. So in such a case the Court would come to the apparently absurd conclusion that the woman had slept with the man but that the man had not slept with the woman. But this absurdity is solely due to the laws of evidence. When a wife makes a confession to a husband in the absence of the corespondent, such a confession is not evidence against him. Nor could it fairly be. It may be a genuine confession or a false one but the corespondent, not being present when it was made, has no chance of testing it at the time. And, as far as the corespondent is concerned, it is pure hearsay. So, if there is no other evidence against him but the judge believes that the confession is a genuine one, he must give the husband a decree but dismiss the corespondent from the suit.

But the Amberley case wasn't in that category at all.

8 In and About a Car

"And was it a wonderful night?" repeated Coventry.

"Yes," said Anne.

"Why?"

"I hadn't been sleeping well."

"It was worth noting in your diary that you'd slept well?"

"If you've ever had insomnia," said Anne, "you'd know the wonderful feeling when you've had a good night—a natural one. It's worth shouting about, and, if there's no one to shout to, put it in your diary."

"But why Michael?" said Coventry.

Anne hesitated for a moment. Then:

"To remind me to write to him or something. I can't remember exactly. And you'll see that 'Michael' is on a different line from 'A wonderful night.' They were quite disconnected thoughts. He had nothing to do with it."

"Are you sure?" asked Coventry.

"Perfectly sure."

"Then why did you hesitate before answering the question?"

"I wanted to think. It's a long time ago. And if someone stole your diary you might hesitate before answering a question on the spur of the moment about an entry you hadn't looked at since you wrote it."

"But don't you think it a very odd coincidence that on the very night that Mr. Brown says Mr. Michael Amberley visited you, you should write down: 'Michael. A wonderful night.' Even on different lines."

"Coincidences do happen," said Anne.

"Of course they do," said Coventry, "but don't you think this is very odd?"

"I can think of many odder things than that in this case," said Anne.

"Such as?"

"Well," said Anne, "the first thing that struck me as odd is that Mrs. Amberley should want a divorce at all, unless she's got a boy friend all lined up to take his place."

"You've no right to say that," said Coventry.

"I've every right," said Anne. "You asked me."

"Don't bicker, you two," said the judge. "You're not married."

I wonder what it would be like if we were, thought Coventry just for a moment. Married to Anne! His own wife had been a pretty girl and was still quite attractive. But Anne was in quite a different class in the beauty stakes. She was a stunner—that was the only word he could think of. He had never made love to such a creature. What would it be like? As for her mind—well, it probably wouldn't be a very quiet home. Stimulating, but not quiet. She certainly wouldn't give him the peace that his wife gave him. Almost perfect peace. What more could a hard-working man want at home than peace? Why should he want to be stimulated? His work surely provided all the stimulus he wanted in life. But what a brain the woman had. It worked like lightning. She'd certainly be at no loss if found almost in the arms of the lodger. She'd have an explanation ready. Stimulating, no doubt, it would be to live with her. But disquieting. His wife would never tell him a real lie. Would Anne ever tell the truth if her purpose required a lie? What madness even to consider it. A weekend perhaps. That would be wonderful. But what about afterwards? If Anne wanted another weekend, she'd stop at nothing to get it. How on earth could he have been such an idiot as to let the thought pass through his mind? There'd be no happiness with Anne. Sensation, yes. Ecstasy, yes. But followed by agony and fear. What a fool. How could he have thought of giving up his permanent happiness, even in what he knew to be a completely fantastic dream? He must get down to the business of the day and demolish this dazzling creature instead of indulging in purposeless daydreams.

"Now, Mrs. Preston," he said, "I want to come to the incident in the car."

"There was no incident in any car," said Anne.

"I am going to ask you to deal with what the inquiry agent says he saw."

"That's quite simple," said Anne. "He didn't see it."

"I'm afraid it's not as simple as that," said Coventry.

"On the contrary," said Anne, "it is just as simple as that. He's a liar and that's all there is to it."

"In spite of what you say," said Coventry, "I must ask you to be good enough to examine his evidence with me in a little more detail."

Anne sighed.

"Oh, well," she said, "if you really think it's worth it."

"Mrs. Preston," said Coventry, "is your case that Mr. Amberley merely stopped the car and kissed you and then drove on again?"

"Yes."

"You never got into the back of the car?"

"There was no need."

"If you'd wanted to have intercourse, there would have been need?"

"You know better than I do, Mr. Coventry. I'm sorry. I shouldn't have said that."

"No, Mrs. Preston," said the judge.

"Did Mr. Amberley pull into a side road?" went on Coventry.

"Certainly not."

"Can you account for the inquiry agent giving a detailed story of the car pulling off the main road, stopping in a side road, of both of you getting into the back of the car, of his creeping up and looking through the rear window and seeing you both?"

"Of course I can. It's his job."

"To commit perjury?"

"If necessary."

"You're very ready to charge other people with perjury when you're the one person who's proved to have committed it."

"What do you expect me to answer to that?" said Anne.

"You say the incident in the car never took place?"

"I certainly do. He wouldn't be the first inquiry agent to have made up a case. If he doesn't get results, he doesn't get any clients."

Coventry paused for a moment. This gave Anne the opportunity to add:

"I told you it wouldn't be worth while."

"Mrs. Preston," said the judge, "it's quite unnecessary to be rude to counsel. He is treating you perfectly courteously. Kindly behave in the same way yourself."

"He has improved," said Anne. "I'll agree to that, my lord."

"Mrs. Preston," said the judge. "If you talk like that again I shall fine you for contempt of court."

"I apologize, my lord," said Anne. "I don't like it here, and I'm afraid it's my way of showing it."

"We've been into all that before," said the judge. "Now let's have no more nonsense."

"Now I want to come to something quite different," said Coventry.

"In that case," said the judge, "I think we'll adjourn."

9 Amberley's Parents

It was a Friday and Amberley went to spend the weekend with his elderly parents in the country. They were both nearly ninety. His father was extraordinarily active for a man of his age. His sight and hearing were good and he was pretty steady on his feet. His mother, on the other hand, was almost blind and very deaf. Moreover, she had various ailments which made her almost bedridden. Yet she was happy.

Until her sight failed her great interest had been reading. And when she could no longer read with her eyes she made use of her prodigious memory to do the reading for her. She would lie in bed happily recalling to herself with astonishing accuracy page after page of her favorite novels. Sometimes, if she realized that someone had come into the room when she was doing this, she would hold up her hand, explaining later that she just wanted to finish the chapter. Sometimes, if asked to do so, she would entertain her husband or visitors by reciting aloud long passages out of the books she loved.

She was once asked by a new doctor if she ever got bored lying in bed.

"Bored!" said the old lady. "With all my books!" Until the explanation was given the doctor thought she was wandering. Neither Braille nor talking books nor any other contrivance could do for a person what her memory did for old Mrs. Amberley. But few have the luck to have a good enough memory and fewer still have the sense to cultivate it. Another of her hobbies was to visit in her mind some of the picture galleries which she had known really well in her more active days. Her one regret was that she could not listen to music. She had always loved listening, but few people (if any) beyond musicians and composers can listen to unheard melodies.

Amberley had wondered very seriously whether to tell his parents about the divorce case. They belonged to a generation and type of family in which divorce was an alien word. The fact that they had never much liked his wife did not really affect the position. Marriage to them was a permanency. On the other hand, if the case were mentioned in the papers his father would certainly learn of it. He made up his mind that it was better to let them know. In any event, he did not like the idea of deceiving them, even if he could succeed in doing so. He decided to tell his father, so that he could pass it on to his mother. When you live with a deaf person of necessity you learn the best method of communicating. Amberley would have had to yell it out and he did not like the idea of that at all, with all the misunderstanding that would probably occur before the truth penetrated. His mother would certainly mishear the word "divorce" for some time.

"I've got some unpleasant news, father," he said when the moment had come.

"Don't suppose it's as bad as you think. Nothing ever is. The doctor told me he had some bad news for me twenty years ago. He should have told it to himself. He's been dead ten years."

"Well," said Amberley, "I hope you're right. Jane has left me."

"She'll come back," said his father. "More's the pity. I never liked her."

"Don't say that, please," said Amberley. "I'm still fond of her. I want her back."

"I'm sorry, my boy," said his father. "I shouldn't have said that. Oh, well, it takes all sorts, and I expect Jane has points which have eluded me."

"She's trying to divorce me."

"Divorce? You're not serious."

"I am."

"But what for? Have they changed the law again? Perhaps you can get divorced now for spilling soup down your shirt. Your mother could have divorced me for that years ago. My father was just as bad. I remember speaking to him about it when I was a young man. 'Your waistcoat is just a mass of stains,' I said. 'I know,' said the old boy. 'You wait till you're my age and yours will be just as bad.' How right he was. You haven't been knocking her about?"

"Of course not."

"I almost wished you'd said you had."

"Please don't, father."

"Well, what is it?"

"She says I've had an affair with another woman."

"Another woman!"

The old man was startled.

"You wouldn't do that," he said.

"No," said Amberley, "I wouldn't."

"Who is she?" said the old man. "Now, what am I saying? Who isn't she? I mean, what's it all about?"

"I met a girl at a hotel," said Amberley, "and a detective says we've slept together."

"A detective? What do you mean? Have you been reading Sexton Blake or something?"

"I had to go to a hotel as Jane wouldn't have me in the house and I met this girl there."

"So there is a girl."

"There is a girl, father, but there's nothing in it."

"D'you like her?"

"Well, yes."

"But that's all?"

"Of course."

"What's this about a detective?"

"Jane employed one to spy on us."

"On us? So you've gone about with the girl?"

"Well, yes."

"But nothing else."

"No, not really."

"What does that mean?"

"Well, I've kissed her."

Amberley's father sighed.

"Oh dear," he said. "The same old story. If you tell me that's all there is to it, I believe you. But who else will?"

"They've got to believe me, father."

"You tell them so," said the old man. "But if a married

man goes about with another girl and kisses her and the detective says there's more to it than that, well, if it weren't you, I'd believe the detective."

"But really, father, people do kiss without going any further."

"Of course they do, but there's got to be a reason. Maybe the girl refuses. Did she refuse?"

"I never asked her."

"Then that isn't the reason. Now I believe you, but that's because I know you. The judge and jury don't know you."

"There isn't a jury, father."

"Well, the judge then. He doesn't know you. Why should he believe you? Why did it stop at kissing? Is that all you wanted?"

Amberley had already been cross-examined very much on these lines by Coventry. He didn't know which he liked the less.

"If you believe me, father, why d'you have to go on questioning me?"

"You're quite right, my boy. I won't say another word. Now, what about your mother? I think we'll leave her till you've won the case. You're going to win it, I hope?"

"So do I, father. I'm sure I will."

"What's the other girl's name?"

"Anne Preston."

"If there were a divorce, would you want to marry her?"

"I've never even thought about it, father."

"Is she good-looking?"

"Well, yes, she is," said Amberley. "She's beautiful."

"I was afraid so," said his father, "but I still believe you. But the judge may think it odd that you didn't sleep with her, unless there's a good reason. But I promised I wouldn't talk about it. Let's go and see your mother."

They went into the old lady's room. She realized that they had come, although she heard nothing. She also realized something else.

"What's the matter?" she asked.

She knew there was no answer. Her son felt he couldn't very well shout "Matter, mother?" For one thing she wouldn't hear what he said and the terrible game of trying to make a deaf person hear would have to be played. But apart from that, there was something the matter and he didn't like pretending to his mother that there wasn't. So Amberley said nothing but his father waited for him to make the first move.

"What's wrong?" repeated Mrs. Amberley.

"Tell her, father," said Amberley.

"It won't be easy," said his father, "but I'll have a go."

He leaned down to her ear and said:

"Jane's left Michael."

The old lady brightened.

"Is that all?" she said. "I thought it was bad news."

"Divorce," said old Mr. Amberley.

"He's going to divorce her, is he?" said the old lady. "Is that necessary? I'm not sure that I like the idea. We've never had a divorce in the family. Till death us do part. Must you, Michael?"

"Tell her I don't want a divorce but that Jane does."

The old man tried but it was difficult.

"But she can't make you divorce her," said the old lady. "Just let her alone. She'll come to her senses. Is there another man?"

"Is there?" repeated the old man.

"There may be," said Amberley, "but I'm not really sure. She seems to like the new manager. But he's very young. Twelve years younger than she is."

"What was that?" said the old lady.

Old Mr. Amberley shook his head. He could never explain that to her. There would be misunderstandings in almost every word. He signaled to the old lady that it was of no importance.

"Not important?" she said. "Of course it's important. Very important. But I'd rather you didn't divorce her, dear. I hope I'm not too narrow-minded, but I just don't like the idea. We'll talk about it another time. Now I must get on with my book. I want to finish the chapter before tea."

On the whole, Amberley felt he'd done as well as he could with his parents, and it was a relief to know that at any rate his father knew what was happening. He went back to London after the weekend with the determination that somehow or other he must prevent a divorce.

10 Respondent and Petitioner

But how could he stop it? He decided to call on Jane. He knew that he was not supposed to do so in the middle of the case and that his own solicitors and counsel would not be pleased if they learned about it. But he was much too concerned with his parents' happiness to worry about legal technicalities. Although neither his father nor his mother had spoken very strongly on the subject, he knew what they must feel. You cannot reason with feeling. If he had wanted to be divorced from Jane he would have controlled his inclinations as long as his parents were alive. Although they made the most of their lives, he knew that he figured largely in their thoughts and that a divorce would be a tremendous blow to them. He hoped he would win the case, but he could make most sure of that if Jane could be persuaded to withdraw it.

He found her alone on the Sunday evening and surprisingly affable.

"You shouldn't be here," she said, "but, as you are, have a drink."

He accepted.

"Cheers," she said.

"Here's luck," he replied.

"D'you mean it?" she said.

"Yes," he said. "I want you to be happy and you need luck to be happy. Yes, I mean it."

"Dear Michael," she said. "You're very nice. It's a pity I can't stand the sight of you."

"What did you say?"

"Skip it. I was only being funny. Why have you come to see me? It's lucky our lawyers can't see us. They'd have a fit."

"That's true enough," he said.

"Well—I'm glad you came," she said. "I've got a proposition to make to you."

"Oh?"

"It'll be much better for everyone if you agree to it. Now I know you're guilty and you know you're guilty but—"

He interrupted.

"I know nothing of the sort," he said.

"Well, I do, anyway," said Jane. "And if I do, you ought to. But I don't mind. Let's assume you don't know it. I shall probably win the case anyway. That you can't dispute."

"I certainly can."

"Well, you can't dispute this. I *might* win it, mightn't I?" she asked.

"Well, I suppose," he agreed reluctantly, "it is possible."

"Now, if I don't win I'm not going to live with you again. So you'll get nothing out of it. Nor shall I."

"My parents hate the idea of a divorce."

"Well, they'll be dead any moment, so they don't really count. Anyway, you can always lie to them."

"I certainly wouldn't."

"Don't be ridiculous. If you can't lie to your parents, who can you lie to? Anyway, let me finish what I was going to say. If you'll give in and let me have my decree, I won't ask for a penny from you, no costs, no maintenance, no anything. I expect I'll have to take an order for costs or it will look like collusion, but I'll never enforce it. Anyway, if you don't trust me, I'll pay £3,000 into your bank and you can pay the costs out of that and keep the change."

"I came here to ask you to drop the proceedings," said Amberley.

"Then you're wasting your time. But my suggestion is a sensible one. It'll give me what I want and won't do you any harm."

"I wouldn't dream of agreeing to it."

"Have another drink."

"No, thank you."

"Look, Michael," said Jane, "I hope you've considered the alternative. If I win—and I can assure you I'm going to—if you haven't slept with that woman, no one's ever slept with anyone and the judge wasn't born yesterday, you know. He looked at me and he looked at her. I hand it to you there. I think she's the most beautiful thing I've ever seen. You've admitted you wanted to sleep with her. Then why didn't you? Scruples? Who's going to believe that? Oh, no, my boy, you're for the high jump all right. But if you'll play it my way it'll be a pretty soft landing."

"I have never slept with Anne Preston," said Amberley emphatically.

"You're not in court now, Michael," said Jane. "Save the histrionics for the judge. Anyway, what's the point of pretending with me?"

"I am not pretending."

"Well, I won't argue with you over that," said Jane. "But do think over what I've said."

"There's nothing to think over."

"Well, if you're going to be pigheaded about it," said Jane, "you may find that you'll be worse off than you imagine."

Amberley said nothing.

"All right," said Jane, "let me warn you of this that, if this case has to go all the way, I'll grind you into the dust. I'll squeeze every penny out of you that I can. I'll send copies of every single newspaper to your parents and—"

"You're a bloody bitch," said Amberley.

"I thought you loved me still," said Jane. "That's not the way to talk to your beloved."

"It's amazing that I do," said Michael, "but that's a thing one can't help."

"Well, if you love me so much, why don't you give me my divorce?"

"You know perfectly well why."

"Well, Michael, you can have it the hard way or the soft way. It's entirely up to you. But I mean what I say. I'll send a cutting from every single newspaper by every post for a month, and, if you don't pay the costs—and they'll be heavy, I assure you—I'll have you bankrupted for them."

"If I let the case go by default," said Amberley, "my parents could see it in the paper anyway."

"They might not," said Jane. "If you were lucky, it mightn't be in the papers they take. After all, no one takes that much notice of divorce these days."

"Anne's picture's been in the paper already."

"Not in the *Times*."

"But the result will be reported there. You and your shops are too well known."

"Suppose I promised to try to buy off the press, would that make any difference?"

"You couldn't. You know you couldn't."

"I could try."

"What's the good of that?"

"If you were likely to win the case," said Jane, "I quite agree that there wouldn't be much point in my talking to you like this. But you're not, Michael, you're not. Don't be so stubborn and refuse to face the facts. Look what you've had to admit. What can any judge say after hearing that and seeing Anne Preston? He's a man, you know, not a computer. You've had her in your arms, you've wanted to sleep with her, Mr. Brown says you have, well, it's pretty obvious, isn't it? And why does she tell lies? Oh, I grant you, no case is over till it's won. Miracles do happen. And that's why I'm prepared to avoid the risk of a miracle by making it easy for you if you'll give in now."

"Well, I won't," said Amberley.

"All right, Michael," said Jane, "if that's how you want it, that's how you shall have it. But I'll see that it hurts you as much as possible and your doting parents as well. Be sensible." She paused. "Now I'll give you one more chance," she added.

Amberley got up and left without saying another word. His visit had been a hopeless failure.

11 Coincidence?

On the Monday morning Coventry was ready to make use of the new material provided by Mr. Brown. He started very warily. First of all he deliberately asked a question which it was difficult for Anne to understand. She asked for it to be repeated.

"I'm so sorry," said Coventry. "It's my fault. We're used to the courts and we forget that you aren't. Is this a new experience for you, Mrs. Preston?"

"A very unpleasant one," said Anne.

"I'm afraid it must be, but have you never been in a court before?" asked Coventry.

"Why should I be asked that?" said Anne. "What's it got to do with the case?"

"That's for his lordship to decide," said Coventry.

"Well, my lord, have I got to answer such questions?"

"How can I tell if it's anything to do with the case unless you do?" said the judge. "Mr. Coventry is on a fishing expedition, I suspect," he added, "and until he pulls in his line no one will know what it's all about."

"I should call it a poaching expedition, my lord," said Tarrington.

"Doesn't that depend upon whether he catches anything?" said the judge.

"It's still poaching, my lord," said Tarrington, "if he's fishing where he shouldn't be, even if he catches nothing."

"Well, you can have one more cast, Mr. Coventry," said the judge.

"Thank you, my lord. Have you been in court before, Mrs. Preston?"

Anne hesitated. After a moment or two she said, "Not a court like this."

"Any court?"

"Yes."

"What sort of court?"

"Your lordship said one more cast," said Tarrington.

"He seems to have caught something, Mr. Tarrington," said the judge. "Suppose you stop playing with it and land it straightaway, Mr. Coventry. I personally don't care for the idea of playing a trout—though I have to admit I enjoy eating them. But I dislike still more the idea of playing a witness."

"I respectfully agree, my lord," said Coventry. "If I had had more definite instructions, this wouldn't have been necessary. But I'll take a chance in view of Mrs. Preston's last answers. It was a magistrate's court, was it not?"

"Yes," said Anne.

"Three years ago were you not charged with indecency with a man in the back of a car parked on the highway?"

"You might add," said Anne, "and were you not acquitted? The answer to both questions would have been yes."

Tarrington got up.

"This is really disgraceful, my lord," he said, "and I must again protest. This is supposed to be cross-examination as to credit. How can it affect my client's credit if she was acquitted?"

"Yes, Mr. Coventry, why should I think the worse of her if she was acquitted?"

"It goes to the proof of this case, my lord," said Coventry. "Three years ago a policeman, or more probably two policemen, swore that Mrs. Preston had behaved improperly with a man in the back of a car. The bench presumably held that the evidence was either deliberately false or mistaken. Three years later a completely different person, Mr. Brown, the inquiry agent, gives similar evidence about a different occasion with a different man. Would it not be an extraordinary coincidence if on *both* occasions the witnesses were lying or mistaken? What is it about Mrs. Preston that induces people to fabricate evidence against her? Or, if they were mistaken on both occasions, what is it she does in the back of a car which makes people think she's being indecent?"

"Don't ask me."

"I want to register a formal protest against the way this case is being conducted by my learned friend," said Tarrington. "It's one of the most shocking performances I've ever seen."

"My learned friend has no right to say that."

"I have every right."

"Is this intended as a personal attack on me?"

"Take it how you like. My client is being subjected to an outrageous cross-examination, my lord, and I ask your lordship to stop it out of hand."

"Well, I will—for ten minutes," said the judge. "I'll rise until you are both cooler."

The judge rose and left. Thereupon Coventry took Tarrington by the arm and they went outside together. Mr. Ringmer followed slowly behind. He was pleased with the result of the last skirmish. Mr. Brown's information had been correct. Anne had been prosecuted and, although she was acquitted, it must be a very extraordinary coincidence indeed that three years later the same mistake should be made again by someone else. Of course, in a way it was hard luck on a person that an *acquittal* should go against her, but Mr. Ringmer found both Mr. Brown's and Coventry's way of arguing the matter very convincing. He hoped the judge would see the matter in the same light.

Everyone left the court except Anne, and, after she had been sitting alone for a short time, Amberley came in.

"Hullo," he said.

"Hullo," said Anne. "What's all this in aid of?"

"I expect the old boy wants a breather," said Amberley.

"I could do with something stronger," said Anne, "a martini, for instance."

"You shall have one at lunch," said Amberley. "I can't tell you how sorry I am about all this. It's horrible what you're having to go through."

"Will there be much more of it?" asked Anne.

"I wish I knew. But, my God! You're wonderful," he said.

"You haven't been here all the time," said Anne.

"You've certainly been wonderful while I have been here."

"I wouldn't call my answer about the kiss so brilliant."

"You were only trying to help."

"But so stupidly. I really don't know what made me do it. I could have kicked myself. After all, it wasn't admitting anything that mattered."

"Well, I think you're splendid. I always shall."

"I'm only defending myself."

"You're defending me too. Bless you. I think you're wonderful."

"Bless you. Well, it's nice to know someone's on my side."

"Isn't the judge?"

"I wonder. But he's a nice old boy. Crusty but fair. Altogether rather a poppet but he's terribly deep."

"You make such a wonderful picture standing up there fighting. Augustus John could have done it justice."

"Or Turner perhaps," said Anne. "The Fighting *Téméraire*."

They laughed.

"If only it would finish," said Amberley. "I think we'll win, don't you?"

"The law's such an odd thing."

"But if we've done nothing wrong," said Amberley, "surely we can't lose." He turned round suddenly and looked at the door. "I thought I heard someone coming in. What an odd sort of court it is. You could catch hold of the judge's gown and give it a tug as he goes in and out."

"What good would that do?"

"It's a bit undignified that you *could*. It's much more impressive when they come in from a door behind the bench. One imagines them going back to a different world altogether to ours. No pubs, no race meetings, no letting your hair down."

"That was a wonderful meeting we went to when you won the tote double."

"Wasn't it? Gay Bessie and Canny Scot."

"Champagne has never tasted so good."

"You shall have a double magnum when this is over—whatever happens."

"Why are you so good to me?"

"Landing you in all this?"

"It's not your fault. More mine than yours."

"Nonsense."

"It's all a bloody shame," said Anne. "I say," she added, "you don't think this place is wired, do you?"

"Wired? Bugged, d'you mean?"

"Yes—and that they've left us together to hear what we say when we're alone?"

"Impossible."

"I wouldn't put it past your beautiful wife or her tame snooper."

"They couldn't do it. This is a public court."

"No, I suppose not. Anyway, as we're not guilty of anything they won't hear us say we were. But it's lucky they never knew about—"

The door opened and Anne stopped abruptly.

Coventry and Tarrington came in and went to their seats. They were soon followed by the associate, the usher, and the judge.

"Go back into the box, please, Mrs. Preston," said Tarrington when the judge was ready to go on.

Anne went back and waited for Coventry's next question.

"Mrs. Preston, have you been talking to Mr. Amberley during the adjournment?"

"Why? Have you been listening?"

"Mrs. Preston," said the judge, "behave yourself and answer the question. Have you been talking to Mr. Amberley?"

"Certainly."

"About the case?"

"Not exactly."

"Have you mentioned the case at all?" asked Coventry.

"I can't remember all we said."

"Did you say anything at all—anything at all about the case?" said the judge.

"We must have said something about it."

"Well, you shouldn't have," said the judge. "A witness under cross-examination mustn't talk to anyone about the case. Didn't you warn her, Mr. Tarrington?"

"Mr. Amberley left the court when I did, my lord," said Tarrington.

"Well, she should have been warned."

"I'm sorry, my lord."

"Well, it's done now."

"Let's see what was done," said Coventry. "What did Mr. Amberley say to you about the case?"

"Well, for one thing he said, if we've done nothing wrong, surely we can't lose."

"And what did you say to that?"

"Didn't you catch?"

"Madam, I was not listening," said Coventry. "My

learned friend will confirm it to you, if necessary. Unlike you and Mr. Amberley, I have an alibi."

"Cut the dramatics, please, Mr. Coventry," said the judge.

"Well," went on Coventry, "what did you say, Mrs. Preston, when Mr. Amberley said as you'd done nothing wrong you couldn't lose."

"Good gracious me, I can't tell you."

"But it's only a few minutes ago. You remember his saying that as you'd done nothing wrong you couldn't lose, surely you must remember why you didn't say, 'Of course we can't' or 'I couldn't agree with you more' or—"

"I hope you wouldn't have used that horrible expression," said the judge.

"I'm afraid I do use it, my lord. But it *is* a horrible expression—I couldn't agree with you—" She checked herself. "I'm sorry, my lord," she added.

"Presumably," went on Coventry, "when Mr. Amberley said what he did *he* might have thought someone was listening? If you thought your conversation was being overheard, he might have thought it."

"I suppose so."

"Well, that would have been a good reason for his saying it, wouldn't it?"

"You mean, to make you think we really were innocent?" said Anne.

"That's right. To make us think you really were innocent. Perhaps that's why he said it."

"He said it because we are innocent."

"So you say," said Coventry. "Tell me, Mrs. Preston, what else did you talk to Mr. Amberley about?"

"I said the law was odd."

"In what particular way?"

"That people who'd done nothing to be ashamed of could find themselves in our position."

"Nothing to be ashamed of? What about the kiss?"

"If that's all they did," interposed the judge, "nearly everyone's kissed someone they shouldn't have at some time."

"Nearly everyone, my lord?" queried Coventry.

"I said nearly everyone. And very few are ashamed of it."

"Well, my lord, if that's your lordship's view—"

"It is and I'm not ashamed of that either."

"To come to another matter," continued Coventry, "what were you saying to Mr. Amberley as we came in, Mrs. Preston?"

"I've no idea."

"Weren't you in the middle of a sentence?"

"It's possible."

"Then why did you stop?"

"If I stopped—and I don't know if I did or didn't—it was because you came in."

"But why? Didn't you want us to hear?"

"Possibly not."

"Why not?"

"I may not have wanted to hurt your feelings."

"You mean you were talking about me?"

"Quite possibly. Would you like to hear what I said about you?"

"I'd like to hear what you said about me," said the judge.

"Well, my lord—"

"No, I didn't mean that," said the judge. "You can say what you like about me behind my back."

"As a matter of fact, my lord, it was rather nice."

"Mr. Coventry," said the judge, "will you get on with your cross-examination, please."

"Certainly, my lord. Mrs. Preston, do you swear that when we came in you weren't starting to say something that might have hurt your case?"

"Certainly I do. I've only once said anything to hurt my case. The stupid lie about the kiss."

"No other lies, stupid or otherwise?"

"Such as?"

"That's for you to tell me."

"How can I remember everything I've said?"

"You can surely remember if you told any other lies."

"None that I can think of."

"But there might be one."

"Yes, there might." She turned toward the judge. "My lord, I'm no more truthful than anyone else, and a good deal less truthful than some, I expect. I'm a woman, my lord, and most of us are inclined to say what suits. It's difficult to be different just because we're in the witness box. That's how I came to be silly about the kiss. I spoke too quickly and then couldn't go back on it."

"But you did go back on it," said Coventry.

"That was after Mr. Amberley gave evidence. I couldn't help myself then, could I?"

"You mean if he hadn't given evidence, you'd have stuck to it?"

"Of course."

"Then there may be other pieces of your evidence which you are sticking to but which are just as untrue?"

"I don't think there are, but there may be."

"That makes it very difficult for me, Mrs. Preston," said the judge. "How am I to pick and choose?"

"You'd know better than I, my lord."

"I'm not so sure."

"But people don't always tell the truth to your lordship."

"No, they don't."

"Even though they've taken an oath to do so."

"You're right there, Mrs. Preston," said the judge. "They ought to change the oath. People swear to tell the truth which they don't know, the whole truth which the laws of evidence don't permit them to divulge, and nothing but the truth which is asking too much of anyone. Witnesses ought to swear to do their best to tell the truth. Don't look at me like that, Mr. Coventry. If I say this often enough in public, something might be done about it. Now let's get on."

"Where from, my lord?"

"That's fair enough. Oh, yes, Mrs. Preston was just instructing me on how to assess the value of her evidence. How am I to know when you're telling the truth, madam?"

"The same as with anyone else, my lord. Other witnesses tell your lordship lies on some matters. The only difference between them and me is that I've admitted it."

"What other lies apart from the kiss?"

"None that matter."

"Let his lordship be the judge of that," said Coventry. "What other lies?"

"I tell you I don't know. It's simply just possible that I said something else too quickly and that it wasn't true. Nothing of great importance."

"Do you not think adultery of great importance?"

"I do in this case."

"Then you don't think it of importance generally?"

"How on earth can I answer such a question? Take a man

who commits adultery with a different woman a dozen times a year or more. Is his adultery on the twelfth occasion important?"

"It's a breach of the Ten Commandments."

"Remember the Sabbath day to keep it holy," said Anne. "Six days shalt thou labor and—"

"That will do, thank you, Mrs. Preston," said Coventry. "Now I'll ask you again. Have you not committed adultery with Mr. Amberley?"

"I have not."

"You're looking at me. Look at his lordship and say it again."

Anne looked at the judge.

"I have not."

"She says it very convincingly, Mr. Coventry," said the judge.

"She said she hadn't kissed him very convincingly, my lord."

"Did she? I don't remember," said the judge. "If I'd known this was coming I'd have made a mental note of it. You know, Mr. Coventry, they'll need films as well as tape recordings in the future. Suppose a witness said something with a wink, it wouldn't show on the tape recorder. I'd like to turn back now and see the expression on Mrs. Preston's face when she said she hadn't kissed him. Can you say you positively remember how she looked when she said it?"

"No, my lord, I can't."

"Can you, Mr. Tarrington?"

"No, my lord," said Tarrington, "but oddly enough I can remember that my learned friend couldn't have told you."

"How so?"

"It just so happens that when he asked the question he

was deliberately looking away from the witness. A trick some of us have, particularly my learned friend."

"I wasn't aware of it. Now, Mrs. Preston," Coventry began, and then realized that he was doing exactly what Tarrington had said—looking away from the witness. He stopped, looked toward Anne, and began again. "Mrs. Preston, I want to come to another episode in your past."

"This is your life, Anne Preston," said Anne.

"Eamon Andrews?" queried the judge. Anne nodded.

"I thought so," said the judge and smiled.

12 In Bed with a Man

"Mrs. Preston," continued Coventry, "do you remember staying with some friends of yours in Scarborough some thirteen years ago?"

"Oh, come," said the judge, "thirteen years!"

"Maybe, my lord," said Coventry, "but the character of the witness is of vital importance in this case."

"Well, I can't stop you."

"Do you remember, Mrs. Preston?"

"The Willoughbys, d'you mean?"

"I don't know the name, but the house was near Scarborough."

"I stayed several times with the Willoughbys there."

"On one of those occasions were you found in the morning by your hostess in bed with a man?"

"Yes."

"Were you married at the time?"

"I was."

"Was it your husband?"

"Yes."

"You swear that?"

"Certainly."

"Then it's not the occasion I'm speaking of."

"That's not my fault," said Anne.

"Was there not an occasion in a house near Scarborough when you were found in bed with a man not your husband?"

"I must think."

"Why do you have to think, if you've never committed adultery?"

"I have never committed adultery," said Anne, "but I still have to think. Yes. I think I know the occasion you're thinking of. Shall I tell you about it? It's rather a long story."

"Were you found in bed with a man not your husband?"

"Might I explain?"

"Answer the question first and then you can explain—if there is any explanation."

"There's an explanation all right but it is rather a long one."

"Please answer the question first."

"It'll make more sense if I give the explanation first."

"Leave his lordship to judge that, Mrs. Preston. Were you not found in bed with a man not your husband?"

"My lord," intervened Tarrington, "I do submit that, if my friend is going into this ancient history, the witness should be entitled to give her answer in her own way."

"Why shouldn't she answer the question first?" said the judge.

"Thank you, my lord," said Coventry. "Well, Mrs. Preston, were you found in . . ."

"Yes, I was."

"And the explanation?"

"Well, it was the Wilkeses who started it," said Anne, "or was it the Willoughbys, I'm not sure, but, whichever it was, they'd been in Buenos Aires—no, that's not true—it was Los Angeles—was it?—really I'm not sure, my lord."

"Perhaps you'd come to the point," interposed Coventry.

"I want to," said Anne, "but I've got to be so careful or you'll say I'm telling lies and take a photograph of me doing so, and then say I looked like that five hundred questions ago or whatever it was. Well, whether it was the Wilkeses or the Willoughbys or whether it was Buenos Aires or Los Angeles—d'you know I've a horrible suspicion it was Paris after all?—well, they'd been staying with the Simpkinsons, the Worcestershire Simpkinsons—the ones with the motto 'I drive slowly but dangerously' . . ."

"Stop!" said the judge. "I can't allow it, Mrs. Preston. I must fine you five pounds." Anne started to look in her bag.

"You can pay later," said the judge.

"Will they take a Diners' card?" said Anne.

"Make it ten pounds, Mrs. Preston," said the judge.

"I shall be frightened to say anything now, my lord."

"Well," said the judge, "if it happens again you'll have to go to prison—after the case is over. Now, if there is any explanation, let's have it in one word."

"Charades," said Anne.

"I beg your pardon?" said Coventry.

"We were playing charades fully dressed."

"If that's true, why couldn't you say so at once?"

"I wanted to play you a bit like you've been playing me."

"You'll find it expensive, Mrs. Preston," said the judge.

"It's rather unfair, my lord. I'm fined for playing him and he gets paid for playing me."

"It's an unfair world, Mrs. Preston, but some kind of order has to be kept in court."

"I suggest to you, Mrs. Preston," said Coventry, "that you're deliberately making this up. Were you not found in bed early in the morning with a man called Stokes after having spent the night with him?"

"I don't know anyone called Stokes."

"Well, whatever his name was, were you not found in bed with him?"

"Not unless you mean my husband or are referring to the charades."

"What was the name of the man you got into bed with fully dressed in the charades?" There was a pause and then Anne said suddenly:

"Oh dear!"

"What's the matter?"

"I just don't know what to say."

"Of course you know what to say. Do you remember his name?"

"Unfortunately I do," said Anne.

"Well, what was it?"

"Well—well—"

"What was it?"

"I'm afraid it was Stokes." The judge looked sternly at Anne. "I'm sorry, my lord," she said, "but I'd completely forgotten, and this was thirteen years ago."

"That's perfectly true," agreed the judge.

"I suggest to you," said Coventry, "that, whether or not charades were played, you and Stokes committed adultery together."

"That's absolutely untrue. I'm sure Mr. Stokes would confirm what I say."

"Where does all this get you, Mr. Coventry?" said the judge. "You have to accept her answers."

"It gets me to another coincidence, my lord. Poor Mrs. Preston. Mistakenly suspected in the back of a car—not once but twice. And when she is found in bed with a man —they're fully dressed playing charades."

13 One for the Price of Two

At this stage in the case both the petitioner and the respondent and Anne could have been forgiven for wondering why it had been necessary for them each to employ two counsel. Coventry and Tarrington appeared to be doing all the work but there were in fact two other counsel engaged in the case. Coventry had a junior called George Litlington while Tarrington's junior was called Caroline Seaford. It is true that before the trial George and Caroline had played a bigger part in the proceedings. They had interviewed their clients and settled all the technical legal documents. But they had done nothing in court, except occasionally whisper to each other or to their respective leaders.

There is at the present moment a move in some quarters to try to alter the rule by which a Q.C. must normally have a junior in every court case. Of course it could be done. If it were, some cases would be done more cheaply and quite as well. Some cases would be wrecked at no less expense than if two counsel had been employed, while the bulk of cases would be done rather more cheaply and rather more inefficiently. In the end the public will get the service it wants. If it wants the best service, it must pay for it. If it is satisfied with a workable, second-rate service, it need not pay as much. The legal world will not come to an end, nor will judges, barristers, and solicitors go on strike, if the movement toward lower costs and less efficiency is successful, but it will simply mean that our inevitably imperfect justice will become rather more imperfect. No human system of justice is perfect or ever will be. Our present system normally involves the presentation by each side of its case by professional lawyers and relies on the belief that, if each case is put forward as well as possible, the result is more likely to be right. Of course it won't always be right. And, of course, one side will sometimes be better represented than the other. But the present method of representation in important or substantial cases is to employ a specialist to do the preliminary work and another specialist to do the work in court. It is expensive. It is not essential. But it works pretty well on the whole. And, if and when it is abolished, mistakes will be more often made and injustices more frequently perpetrated.

George and Caroline had very different qualities. George, who was forty-four at the time, was cheerful, philosophic, conservative, unimaginative, hard-working, and quite able. Caroline, who was much younger, had a very inquiring mind. George would never have thought of asking Anne as his first question, if he had been cross-examining: "Why

didn't you commit adultery with Mr. Amberley?" Caroline
might well have done so. She had grown up to accept nothing that was not satisfactorily established. As a child she
had always resented the "Why-mustn't-I?"—"Because-I-
say-so" rule so firmly established in some families. George,
on the other hand, would as a boy state with absolute confidence anything his father might have told him. He would
even have repeated that the Battle of Hastings was in 1065
if his father in a leg-pulling mood had told him so with
apparent seriousness. "I know all the books say 1066, but
they're wrong, George. You tell your master to go to the
British Museum and look up a very old book called *De
Pugna Hastigiense*. It was published about 1402. There
you'll find the date is given as 1065. And the reason for the
mistake of calling it 1066 is also given. I forget what it
was. But the book didn't have a big enough circulation.
They didn't have Penguins in those days. So everyone says
1066."

George's father would not in fact have involved his son
in such embarrassment but, had he done so, George would
have gone into battle as confidently and unsuccessfully as
Harold. Caroline would never have been caught that way.
She would have asked her father to take her to the British
Museum first and so eventually would have called his bluff.
Not because she would have actively disbelieved him in the
first instance but simply because she wanted to see for herself. Her parents realized at a very early age that it was much
too dangerous to make wide general statements about re-
ligion, politics, books, plays, or people in front of Caroline
without having a very cogent reason with which to back up
their pronouncements. The result was that in Caroline's
household inaccurate general pronouncements were very

few. When they were made they were usually provoked by annoyance and soon regretted. How can you explain to an intelligent inquiring child of fourteen why an act of Parliament, the terms of which you do not fully know or understand, should not have been passed? A dose of Caroline Seaford made for clear thinking and would be good for many households.

When she at first interviewed Anne she had asked her quite a number of the questions which Coventry had asked. But when she asked them they were designed not to embarrass her client but to elicit the truth. At the end of the conference Anne asked her what she thought. Caroline was not frightened of expressing her opinions quite definitely. From an early stage in her career she appreciated that, when she was asked for her opinion, it was her opinion and not her doubts which were wanted. She was always definite and usually right.

"What do I think?" she said. "That, of course, depends on whether I believe you, Mrs. Preston. You want the truth, I suppose?"

"Of course."

"I wonder. Everyone says that, but most people simply want to be encouraged. And it's the judge's opinion that matters, not mine, in a case like this. Well, Mrs. Preston, I can't say that I believe everything you say, but I do believe that the charges against you are unfounded."

"Well, if you believe it, shouldn't the judge?" asked Anne.

"He doesn't get the same opportunity," said Caroline. "I see you in quiet in my chambers. There's no hurry. I can ask you anything I like and, if you're wise, you tell me the truth. The atmosphere in court is quite different. Of course it cuts both ways. Sometimes what appears to be the truth in the peace of the Temple seems very far removed from it in the bitter struggle in court. Sometimes the truth has an unpleasant habit—unpleasant from some people's point of view—of coming out in court. So I can't be at all certain what will happen in court. But you ask me if I believe that you didn't commit adultery, and my answer is that I do."

"That's very gratifying," said Anne.

"It will be much more gratifying to both of us," said Caroline, "when the judge says it."

The conference between George and Jane Amberley had been very different. He asked her few searching questions and gave her no definite opinion as to the probable result of the case.

"My dear Mrs. Amberley," he said, "if I could forecast the result of every case I think I'd sell forecasts outside the law courts instead of presenting cases inside. As a matter of fact I believe that there'd be quite a sale from them, what with the present trend for horoscopes. Look how well some of the racing tipsters do. And what do they know? As often as not it's a gamble. So it is in court sometimes. I've a good idea. How about offering the result of a case—no win, no fee? The man who wins would be so pleased that he'd willingly pay quite a bit on his way out. And sometimes you'd come out all right even if you told someone he'd lose. He might in consequence agree to quite a satisfactory settlement. He'd be so pleased that on his way out he might well put something in your box. What d'you think of that, Mrs. Amberley?"

"What do I think of it?" said Jane. "I cannot tell you my honest opinion in polite language. But I will say that it sounded more like a music hall comedian talking—and a not very funny one—than a barrister whom I had engaged over a very serious case."

"So sorry," said George, not in the least put out. "I do apologize. My cheerfulness will keep breaking in. But to be perfectly serious, no case is won or lost until the judge has given judgment. You may succeed or you may fail. As Mr. Ringmer has, I think, told you, everything will depend upon how your husband and Mrs. Preston stand up to cross-examination. If they do well, then I'm afraid you're likely to fail for lack of sufficient evidence. But if they do badly, then you should win. And I'm bound to say that in briefing Charles Coventry, as Mr. Ringmer tells me he's going to, you will have the best possible chance of success. I can only say that, if I had a case of my own in which cross-examination was important, I should like to have Coventry on my side and not against me."

"That's something," conceded Jane. "I've got to win this case," she added. "If there's anything else you can think of to help me, you do it. You and Mr. Ringmer. I don't care what it costs. I've got to win."

"We shall do all we can," said George.

Caroline and George had lunch together just after Coventry had dealt with the charades incident.

"What do you make of it?" George asked.

"It's very odd," said Caroline. "I got the feeling during that last incident that 'charades' was the right word to use, that that's what we were playing and that it wasn't a genuine case at all."

"Well, I'm glad it's not," said George. "You don't get paid for charades. But it is a bit odd, I grant you. Though divorce cases are often like that. Who knows what happens between husband and wife except the wife and the husband? I was really quite upset—well, perhaps upset is too strong a word but I got quite worked up about one of the first cruelty petitions I saw. The things the husband was supposed to have done to his wife, set fire to her night-dress, thrown her out the window, half-strangled her, threatened her with a revolver, tried to drown her. Then I came to the husband's side of the case. It was almost worse than the wife's. She was said to have bitten him, shot him through the arm, jabbed a needle into him, and thrown a kettle of boiling water over him. All this over a period of five years during which they'd had three children. There was nothing in any of the incidents except the kettle. She *had* thrown the contents of a kettle of lukewarm water over him. All the other incidents had a perfectly good explanation. But, to anyone who doesn't know the form, many cruelty petitions would make them think they were dealing with monsters, not men and women."

"But what about the shooting?"

"Oh, that. Well, yes, she had shot him, but it was obviously a pure accident. There were letters between them while he was in hospital which showed that quite plainly."

"The biting?"

"Just fun and games."

"I suppose he sat on the needle?"

"Exactly."

"D'you think there are any Willoughbys?" asked Caroline.

"There must be," said George, "though we never had the name."

"Your Mr. Brown got the dope, I suppose?"

"Yes."

"Funny he didn't get the name."

"He got Stokes," said George.

"Oh, yes, of course, Stokes," said Caroline. "But I must say I didn't believe any of it. It was all like a dream."

"Well," said George, "I know what you mean. But if our man gets information that Mrs. Preston was found in bed with a man in Yorkshire, and she agrees that there is some truth in it, well, something must have happened. Whether it was charades or not is another matter. But she was found in bed with a man."

"I suppose so," said Caroline. "Of course we didn't know anything about this until Coventry started cross-examining her about it."

"Quite."

"She seemed so happy about it that it's difficult to think there was something sinister in it."

"That may be just her way of getting rid of suspicion," said George. "She's a fly customer."

14 Consultation

It was because Coventry was also of the opinion that Anne was a fly customer that he called a conference that evening to discuss one or two points. Mr. Ringmer and George Litlington and Jane Amberley were present. Coventry had been tempted to have Mr. Brown there too but, on the whole, considered that there was no sufficient reason for not conforming to the rule of not seeing witnesses. It is probably a sensible rule and is in effect designed to prevent witnesses from being coached by counsel. It does not, however, prevent counsel from interviewing the person who in most cases is the most important witness of all, the lay client. In fact in the Amberley case Mrs. Amberley did not appear to be in the least an important witness. She could give no evidence against her husband at all. Anne and Amberley, on the other hand, were vital witnesses for the defense and Tarrington was fully entitled to interview them and did so on several occasions.

Coventry wanted Jane present in case there was any

further material she might provide for the purpose of demolishing Anne.

"Well, Mr. Ringmer," he said when they were all seated, "has Mr. Brown got anything more for us?"

"Not at the moment, I'm afraid," said Mr. Ringmer.

"He's an extraordinary fellow," said Coventry. "There's nearly always something in what he brings along. I must confess I've the greatest difficulty in believing anything he says on the face of it—yet, when you get down to it, if it doesn't turn up trumps it turns up something."

"I really don't know why you say you don't believe him, then," said Jane. "I was assured that he was one of the best known inquiry agents."

"He's known all right," said Coventry. "That's one of the troubles about him. You never know whether what he turns up with is a cock-and-bull story or almost true. And he himself would tell a lie as soon as look at you."

"It's a pity I didn't know this before," said Jane.

"Well, so far he hasn't done so badly," said Coventry. "Both his stories about Mrs. Preston had some basis to them. It's a pity she wasn't convicted. All the same the judge must think it's odd that this is the second case against her in a car. Now what else have we got? I shall be running out of material soon, and she isn't down yet."

"She's got to be, Mr. Coventry," said Jane.

"Mr. Coventry is doing all he possibly can, Mrs. Amberley," said Mr. Ringmer. "If I may say so, sir, it's been a most brilliant performance. The way you've rattled her from time to time by the sheer unexpectedness of your questions has been a revelation to me."

"The trouble is," said Coventry, "that she isn't really on the run yet. She's been shaken up once or twice, and I've got a couple more things for her, but we've got to sink her without trace. Just making her heel over won't do."

"I suppose a letter wouldn't be any good," said Jane.

"A letter? How d'you mean, Mrs. Amberley?" asked Coventry.

"A letter I wrote her."

"When did you do this?"

"Soon after Michael left me."

"Have you a copy?"

"Well, I had but I haven't been able to find it."

"What did it say?"

"Well, it asked her to keep away from him."

"It asked her to keep away from him?" repeated Coventry questioningly.

"Yes."

"But why?" asked Coventry. "If you wanted to get rid of him, the nearer she got to him the better."

"Who said I wanted to get rid of him?"

"Well, he says you turned him out of the house."

"Of course he does. But it isn't true. We had a row and he left."

"Did you want him back?"

"Of course I did. That's why I wrote this letter."

"But you don't want him back now?"

"Not second hand, no, thank you. I wouldn't have him back now on any terms whatever. I hate the sight of him."

"But that wasn't so when he left?"

"Of course it wasn't."

"What's happened to make such a difference?"

"What's happened? What's happened?" repeated Jane scornfully. "He's slept with Mrs. Preston. That's what's happened. Perhaps you wouldn't mind if your wife slept with the milkman. Well, that's up to you. It takes all sorts. I can only tell you, Mr. Coventry, that once my husband goes with another woman, that's it. If I hadn't a penny to my name and he offered me a million pounds I wouldn't have him back. He's made his bed with her and he can share it with her. Or with anyone else for all I care. The one thing that's certain is that he won't share it with me. That's flat."

"But when he left, you'd have liked him to come back?"

"Certainly," said Jane. "I don't know why you should have any doubt about it. Look, Mr. Coventry, I was brought up on the Ten Commandments. They mean something to me. It's the seventh, isn't it? Well, I know most people don't mind about such things these days, but I do, like my parents before me. And once Michael broke that, he was out as far as I was concerned."

"There is a suggestion, Mrs. Amberley," said Coventry, "that you had your eye on the new manager."

"I had my eye on the new manager!" repeated Jane. "Well, of course I did. If I didn't have my eye on him how would I know what sort of a manager he was? You've got to watch everybody in my business from the sweeper to the manager. But you're quite right, I did like the look of him. I still do. You can like someone without breaking your marriage vows, can't you? I'll tell you something else. If I win this case—I should say when I win it—because you've got to win it for me—I may marry him. That's right, marry him. Don't look so surprised. What's wrong with it? It would never have happened if Michael hadn't started it. I can take a liking to someone without rushing into his arms, can't I? Have you never looked across the street and said to yourself that you'd like to go to bed with that woman? But you don't do it, do you? Nor do I. So long as I'm married to Michael, I'll stay clean. The same as he should. If he'd behaved himself, this would never have happened."

"Well, what about this letter?" said Coventry when Jane stopped at last. "What actually did it say?"

"It said I'd be glad if she'd keep away from my husband, that he was still married to me and that I didn't like trespassers. But those weren't the actual words."

"Did you get any reply?"

"Not a thing."

"Where did you send it?"

"To her flat."

"How did you know her address?"

"Mr. Brown gave it to me."

"But why was Mr. Brown on the scene by then?"

"Are you on his side or on mine?" asked Jane.

"On yours, of course," said Mr. Ringmer. "But Mr. Coventry has to ask you these questions."

"Oh, he does, does he?" said Jane, "Well, the answer to that one is very simple. I didn't trust Michael. I thought he was up to something."

"You didn't trust him but you wanted him back?" asked Coventry.

"Certainly," said Jane. "I might have been wrong. I hoped I *was* wrong. But I wasn't going to be made a fool of. So I employed Mr. Brown."

"As soon as your husband left you?"

"As soon as he left me. If Mr. Brown had given him a clearance, no one would have been happier than me. But he didn't give him a clearance. He gave him the thumbs down. So it's thumbs down for me too."

"So you sent the letter to prevent anything happening?" asked Coventry.

"Exactly," said Jane. "I'm glad you're beginning to understand. It's taken a bit of time, I must say."

"So you sent the letter to her flat and had no reply?"

"Yes."

"Can you be sure she got it?"

"Well, it didn't come back to me."

"Can you remember the exact terms of your letter?"

"Very nearly."

"Tell me then."

"Well, it was headed 'Trespassers will be prosecuted.' That was underlined in red. 'Dear Mrs. Preston,' it said, 'please keep off the grass. Yours sincerely, Jane Amberley. P.S. My husband is the grass.'"

"Well, that's very interesting," said Coventry. "I wonder what Mrs. Preston will say?"

"Wonder what she'll say?" said Jane. "Don't be soft. She'll say she never had it. Then where are you? That's why I didn't mention it before. Didn't think it would help. D'you still want me to look for the copy?"

"Oh, yes, please," said Coventry. "I suppose it was handwritten."

"Well, you suppose wrong," said Jane. "I typed it on an office machine, so that I could have a copy easier."

"So the copy's typewritten, if you can find it?"

"That's an idea," said Jane. "I could easily make another, and say it's the original. No one would know the difference."

"They would, if Mrs. Preston produced the letter."

"If she produced the letter," said Jane, "it wouldn't matter what the copy was, and I could always say I'd made a mistake and forgotten that I'd lost the original carbon and typed another out later."

"Why a carbon then?"

"You're right," said Jane. "I'll do both. Top and carbon."

"I'm afraid not," said Coventry. "I wouldn't dream of letting you pretend that a copy produced by you was the original carbon."

"How are you to know?" said Jane. "If I tell you it's the original carbon, you can't tell whether it is or not."

"That's true," said Coventry, "but I can only ask you to tell me the truth about it. I shall have to accept your word."

"Well, you can," said Jane. "I told you, I'd mislaid it. That's true. But what's lost can be found. Ever heard of the prodigal son?"

Coventry had never liked Jane but by the time the conference was over he disliked her very much indeed. He couldn't help sympathizing with Amberley for preferring Anne, if that was the truth of the matter. But he was far too experienced a practitioner to allow his dislike of his client to alter his determination to win the case, if it could be won by proper means. Fortunately barristers and solicitors are quite as able at controlling their feelings toward their patients as are doctors and dentists. One never hears of a dentist pulling out the wrong tooth because he disliked the patient or a doctor getting the nurse to leave a couple of swabs in just to tease the beggar. If barristers at the criminal bar had to like their clients before they would defend them properly, very few criminals would get a fair trial. Coventry did, however, think for a moment or two that he'd much prefer to be on the other side and appearing for Anne. Though, he reflected, on the whole, it was just as well he wasn't.

15 The Carbon Copy

It was just as well. Jane had been perfectly right when she asked Coventry if he hadn't looked across the street and seen somebody he'd like to go to bed with. Like many faithful husbands, he had. Some husbands stay faithful from habit, some from lack of opportunity, some from expediency, and a few from moral principles. Coventry had never examined the reason or reasons why he had never strayed. He was devoted to his wife and children, but, except in the case of a few individuals, this cannot blind a man to the attractions of another woman. It is trite to say that men are naturally polygamous. Trite but true. The reason that people in Coventry's position do occasionally get involved in divorce proceedings is normally pure selfishness. It is easy enough for an intelligent man and woman to recognize at a very early stage danger signs in a new acquaintanceship. At that stage it is easy enough to break off the acquaintanceship. But sometimes from pure selfishness neither of the persons involved will do so. And then the trouble begins. Coventry realized that it was far better that Anne should not be his client lest in a middle-aged moment he should act selfishly and be sorry afterwards. Far better to have his unspoken affair with her in court and never to see her again. He would occasionally have lingering regrets, but after a short time not much more than those for the charming woman who sat next to them in the Spanish Bar at Fortnum and Mason, to whom he passed the sugar and for whose thank-you smile he would have done much more.

"You seem very cheerful this morning," his wife said at breakfast.

"I am," said Coventry, "for two reasons."

"Oh?"

"First, or possibly second, the case I'm on is quite intriguing and everything depends on my cross-examination."

He paused.

"And the second or should I say first?"

"I'm cross-examining a woman and I've fallen in love with her."

"What's she wearing?" asked his wife.

"I haven't the faintest idea."

"Well, what's she look like?"

"Ravishing. As a matter of fact, there was a picture of her in the *Mirror* or something. You may have seen it."

"I must find it. Are you going to ask her in for a drink? Oh, no, of course you can't. She's on the wrong side. What a pity. It would be nice to have a rival. You'd have to give me a new brooch or something to help me compete."

"No one will ever compete with you," said Coventry.

His wife looked at him sharply.

"Good gracious!" she said. "You're almost serious. I thought you were being funny."

"Well, I am and I'm not. She really is terrific. Not just to look at. But her mind. She fights like a Tartar. I have to watch her, I can tell you. She's brilliant. It's quite a new experience. And all the more satisfactory that nothing can come of it."

"I'll say," said his wife. "I think I'll come to court and see her. Any reason why I shouldn't?"

"None at all. I'd like you to. I hope you'll think it's a compliment when you see her. No one could object to being compared to her."

"Am I like her, then?"

"No. I didn't really mean compare. To run in the same race, I suppose I meant. Most entrants would withdraw on seeing her."

"Perhaps I will."

"You can't. You've won already."

"That's lucky."

"Very. For me," said Coventry. "She's beautiful and brilliant but she's an absolute shocker. How awful to be married to someone you can't trust an inch."

"Why isn't she married?"

"She's a widow."

"How long ago did he die?"

"Six years or so."

"That's rather a long time."

"I agree. I can't understand it. But by Jove she'd lead anyone a dance. I shouldn't care for it."

"What would you care for then?"

"You come along this morning and see."

"I will. I'll come with you."

So when Coventry renewed his cross-examination his wife was there to watch. Before the judge came in Mr. Ringmer gave a document to Coventry.

"She's found it," he said. "This is the carbon."

Coventry looked at it. Its condition was such that it might be a genuine carbon copy or might have been made the same morning and creased a little.

"Let me speak to her," said Coventry.

Mr. Ringmer went out and fetched Jane from the corridor.

"Mrs. Amberley," said Coventry, "is this the actual carbon of the letter you sent to Mrs. Preston?"

"Certainly it is."

"Where did you find it?"

"With some other letters and copy letters."

"You are quite sure that this is the original carbon copy, Mrs. Amberley?" asked Coventry, laying particular emphasis on the word "original."

"It would serve you right if it weren't," said Jane. "But I happen to be telling you the truth. I dare say most of your clients don't. That's why you're so suspicious."

"Very well, I'll put it to her," said Coventry, "and we'll see what she'll say."

"I've told you what she'll say," said Jane. "She'll deny it completely."

"You seem very confident of that," said Coventry.

"Well, I haven't been sitting in this court watching her lie for nothing. It's just her word against mine. I expect I'd do the same myself if I were in her position. I can't prove the letter was posted. And even if I could it doesn't mean it was delivered."

A few moments later the judge came in and Anne went into the witness box. Coventry's wife looked at her with great interest. Her husband was right. At least he wasn't. Hardly any woman could compete with Anne either in her looks or in the way she wore them. And her clothes were perfect too. She may be a shocker, thought Mrs. Coventry, but I'm damned glad she didn't meet Charles before me. I don't blame him.

"Mrs. Preston," began Coventry, "I want you to look at this document."

"Another one stolen by your snooper?" said Anne.

"No, Mrs. Preston," said Coventry. "This is a copy of a letter sent to you."

"Couldn't he find the original when he broke in?" asked Anne.

"Now that's enough of that," said the judge. "I don't blame you in the least for being indignant about that episode. So am I. But it's no use going on about it. Kindly look at the letter."

The usher handed it to Anne, who looked at it.

"What's this supposed to be?" she asked.

"A copy of a letter sent to you by Mrs. Amberley."

"Rubbish," said Anne.

"I told you so," whispered Jane to Mr. Ringmer.

"I've only had one letter from Mrs. Amberley and this isn't it."

"Where is the letter?"

"I haven't kept it."

"What was the effect of it?"

"It was a silly letter I thought. It said something about her being the wife of a man I was seeing something of and she didn't mind provided I was serious."

"She didn't mind provided you were serious?" repeated Coventry.

"Something of that sort," said Anne. "Not the actual words of course."

"Forgive me a moment, my lord," said Coventry and whispered to Jane:

"What d'you say about this?"

"This is the only letter I sent her," said Jane.

"Are you sure?"

"Absolutely."

"Mrs. Preston," said Coventry, "I want you to be very careful about your evidence in this matter."

"I'm always very careful about my evidence."

"Are you? What about the kiss?"

"Oh, that," said Anne. "All right, except for the kiss. Does that satisfy you more?"

"It doesn't matter whether it satisfies me or not," said Coventry.

"But I like satisfying you," said Anne.

Mrs. Coventry was glad that Anne would not be coming round for a drink.

"Stop it, Mrs. Preston," said the judge. "I've already had to fine you once. I don't want to do so again."

"I suggest to you that it is quite untrue that my client ever sent you a letter to the effect you mention," said Coventry.

"I can't stop you making suggestions to me, but I can only say that she did."

"Has my client sent you one letter or more than one?"

"One."

"Well, we're agreed about that," said Coventry. "Was the letter typewritten or handwritten?"

"Typewritten."

"You will notice that the document I handed to you is typewritten."

"Yes," said Anne. "I did notice that."

"It is a carbon copy of a letter sent to you by Mrs. Amberley."

"It is not. It's a forgery."

"I'll give you one more chance to change your evidence."

"I've no intention of changing it."

"That document you hold in your hand was typed out on a typewriter in my client's office."

"I don't doubt it," said Anne. "Last night, by any chance?"

"Don't be offensive, madam," said Coventry.

Tarrington rose.

"As a matter of fact, my lord," he said, "this document has never been disclosed to my client and for all the petitioner's affidavit discloses it might have been typed last night."

"Why was it not disclosed, Mr. Coventry?" asked the judge.

"It was only discovered last night," said Coventry.

"Discovered, not typed, Mr. Coventry?" asked the judge.

"Certainly, my lord. My client says and will if necessary give evidence later that this is the original carbon copy."

"Kindly read it out, Mrs. Preston," said Coventry.

Anne read it out.

"Rather striking language, don't you think?" asked Coventry.

"Not particularly," said Anne.

"Do you swear that you did not have the original of that carbon copy?"

"There never was an original, not sent to me anyway."

"You're sure of that?"

"Not as far as I can remember."

"Surely you'd remember a letter in those terms?"

"Very likely."

"Has anyone else ever written to ask you to keep away from her husband?"

"No one has ever written to ask me to keep away from her husband."

"Do you find that many letters addressed to you go astray?"

"How can I tell? If they go astray, I don't get them."

"But the person who's written to you may write again or speak to you."

"Well, I don't remember any."

"For the last time, is not this the carbon of the letter you received?"

"It is not," said Anne. "Would it convince you if I produced you the original?"

"I beg your pardon?" said Coventry.

"Oh, I know," said Anne, "you are going to say that a moment ago I said I hadn't kept it. But now I come to think of it, I think I have it still."

"Where?"

"In my hotel."

"Where is your hotel?" asked the judge.

"Just across the Strand, my lord."

"Hadn't she better go and get it, then?" asked the judge.

"Certainly," said Coventry, "if she can. But before she goes, let us be clear about what she is fetching. What is it you think you may have in your hotel?"

"A letter from Mrs. Amberley."

"Typewritten or handwritten?"

"Typewritten."

"And roughly what does it say?"

"I've told you. She didn't mind about me and her husband if it was serious."

"There's no such letter," said Jane out loud.

"Silence," said the usher.

"You can say 'silence' as much as you like," said Jane, "but there's no such letter."

"Mrs. Amberley," said the judge, "you must not talk like that. Mrs. Preston, will you kindly go and fetch the letter."

"Certainly, my lord."

"Be as quick as you can, please."

Anne left the witness box and the Court.

"While we're waiting, my lord," said Coventry, "I wonder if I might ask Mr. Amberley some more questions."

16 Another Brief Encounter

"Any objection, Mr. Tarrington?" asked the judge.

"None at all, my lord," said Tarrington, "but I'll be glad when my friend finishes thrashing about trying to extract a case for himself from somewhere."

"That's quite unjustifiable. I've established a very strong case," said Coventry.

"You've done nothing of the sort," said Tarrington.

"Haven't I got something to say about this?" said the judge.

"Of course, my lord," said Coventry.

"Certainly, my lord," said Tarrington.

"Well, I'm not saying it—till later," said the judge. "Come along, Mr. Amberley."

Amberley went into the witness box. "You're still on oath, you know," the judge reminded him.

"Mr. Amberley," said Coventry, "when we came in after the short adjournment you and Mrs. Preston were talking to each other."

"I was not aware that we shouldn't."

"That may be, but would you please tell me as accurately as possible what was being said as we came in. I think Mrs. Preston was speaking."

Amberley hesitated. "It's a little difficult to remember exactly," he said.

"I dare say, but please do your best."

"So much has happened."

"No doubt, but what happened between you and Mrs. Preston as we were coming in?"

"Well, nothing happened. I don't quite follow."

"What was being said?"

"We talked about a lot of things."

"What was being said by Mrs. Preston as we came into court?"

"Well, er—as a matter of fact—it was something I didn't understand. I may have misheard," said Amberley.

"What did you *think* she said?"

"Well, I thought she said 'It's lucky they never knew about—' and then you came in."

"I see. To what was she referring?"

"I haven't the faintest idea."

"Not the faintest idea?"

"None at all. I've been trying to think ever since what she can have meant."

"Is there any occasion we don't know about when you and Mrs. Preston were together?"

"Of course," said Amberley. "We met a good deal in the hotel."

"I mean when you were alone together."

"Well, we've been to the races together, we went to the theater once, and we dined together in town."

"When was that?"

"I don't know exactly, but Mrs. Preston was going abroad. She was taking the night flight, and I drove her to town. We dined and went to the theater and I drove her to the airport."

"Have you no idea when it was?"

"The actual date? No. I've a hopeless memory for dates and I don't keep a diary. But Mrs. Preston could tell you for certain."

"No doubt."

"You shouldn't sneer, Mr. Coventry," said the judge. "Her passport will show it."

"Exactly, my lord," said Amberley.

"Mr. Tarrington," said the judge, "kindly get your solicitor to telephone through to Mrs. Preston's hotel and ask her to bring her passport with her if she has it."

"Very good, my lord."

Tarrington's solicitor got up and walked out.

"But there's nothing to be ashamed of in those incidents, Mr. Amberley?" went on Coventry.

"Nothing at all."

"Then to what could Mrs. Preston have been referring?"

"It's a mystery to me."

"It's a mystery altogether because Mrs. Preston says she was saying something else when we came in."

"She made a mistake. I don't know if I'm allowed to say this, my lord . . ."

"What is it?" asked the judge.

"Well, she's been in the witness box for some time and it's not easy being cross-examined like this, even though we've done nothing wrong. And women are such odd creatures, my lord. They don't always think before they speak."

"You think Mrs. Preston isn't a very reliable witness?" asked Coventry.

"I think she's absolutely reliable on the main matters," said Amberley, "but she may get flustered or annoyed or have a false sense of loyalty toward me, and sometimes may answer too hastily and then be frightened to back out of it."

"You're standing up for Mrs. Preston very nobly, Mr. Amberley. Are you fond of her?"

"Fond? Yes. In love, no."

"Have you ever been in love with her?"

"No."

"You said you'd have liked to sleep with her."

"That's true."

"You don't have to be in love with a woman to want to sleep with her? Fondness will do?"

"I suppose so."

"You were fond of Mrs. Preston?" continued Coventry.

"Yes, but we did not commit adultery."

"You've still no idea what Mrs. Preston can have been referring to?"

"No idea at all."

"But she was apparently referring to something she didn't want us to hear."

"It sounded like it."

"That is all I wish to ask, my lord," said Coventry.

"Well," said the judge, "if there's nothing else we can get on with, I'll rise till Mrs. Preston gets back." The judge rose and went out. Finally there was no one left except Coventry and Tarrington.

"Coming to have a smoke?" said Coventry.

"No, I'm smoking too much."

"So am I. This is an odd affair, don't you think?"

"Very," said Tarrington.

"Your Mr. Amberley doesn't seem a bad chap at all."

"That's what's so odd. They're in this together—or they're not. Yet I'd believe Amberley implicitly if it weren't for the woman."

"I'm not sure that I'd believe him," said Coventry, "but he's certainly a good witness. Perhaps a little too good to be true. But your Mrs. Preston's not bad either, as a matter of fact, except for one little failing."

"Which is?"

"A complete disregard for the truth."

"Oh—come," said Tarrington. "That's going a bit far. She admitted to her one lie."

"Only when she had to. She just says anything to suit her case. She's clever up to a point, I grant you. But completely unscrupulous."

"What about your client?"

"What was wrong with her?"

"This letter Mrs. Preston's gone to fetch."

"You mean, my woman may have forged the so-called copy?"

"Yes," said Tarrington.

"Far too risky. She couldn't tell if your woman had kept the original. At any rate, if she has got it and produces it, it'll sink one of them."

"But what's the point of Mrs. Preston pretending she's got a different letter at home if she knows she hasn't?"

"I must admit that I don't entirely understand your client's mentality," said Coventry.

"No, I don't think you do. But you rather like her all the same."

"What are you talking about?"

"I know you, old boy. She's made quite an impact on you."

"Don't be ridiculous."

"Well, what do you think? What'll my woman come back with?" said Tarrington.

"Nothing, and a lame explanation that she's lost the letter. If the judge doesn't find adultery proved, I'll eat my hat. I'd be prepared to believe Amberley if it were only the inquiry agent against him, but your lady sinks him like a stone. Old Brace is no fool."

"He's being quite nice to her on the whole," said Tarrington.

"That's when he's most dangerous. He's always nice to the people he's going to down."

"But he fined her ten pounds."

"That's nothing. He had to keep his end up. But I've noticed it time and again with him—and with other judges too. 'Sit down, madam. Have a glass of water, madam.' 'Don't bully the witness, Mr. Coventry.' 'I think that was a very fair answer, Mr. Coventry.' 'I entirely agree with you, madam.' But when it comes to judgment, 'I don't believe a word madam says. Madam is one of the most prevaricating witnesses I've had the misfortune to come across. I do not like branding anyone a liar, but I have no hesitation in saying that that's what madam is.' Oh, no, my dear fellow, don't lower your guard because of his pretty little ways."

"So you think he'll down us?"

"Are you a betting man?"

"No, not really."

"Good. I'll lay you two to one she doesn't come back with the letter and, whether she comes back with it or not, three to one I'll win."

"What in?"

"You choose the weapons."

"Pounds," said Tarrington.

"Who was it said 'guineas are handsomer'? A Lord Chancellor, wasn't it?"

"Guineas it shall be. It was Lord Macclesfield and he went to jail. No, it was his secretary."

"Jail for perjury is where your client may land herself if she's not careful," said Coventry. "No, Macclesfield went to the Tower. She'd look rather impressive on one of the battlements staring out to freedom along the Thames."

"What was I saying half a minute ago?"

"Just because I can see she's a good-looking woman, that doesn't mean I want to sleep with her."

"How could you in open court?"

Very softly Tarrington began to sing:

> "Out in the open with everyone passing
> With everyone passing and shouting what ho!"

Coventry then joined him:

> "Martha a cab-horse they took off her harness
> So what does it matter, I'd . . ."

At that moment the door opened and Anne looked in. Slightly startled at what she saw and heard she withdrew again. Coventry and Tarrington stopped abruptly like schoolboys. A moment later Anne came in again.

"I'm sorry," she said. "I thought I'd come to the wrong place."

"We'll send for the judge," said Coventry.

Tarrington immediately went out, leaving Anne and Coventry alone.

There was a moment's silence.

"Am I allowed to talk to you?" asked Anne.

"I've never thought about it," said Coventry. "But I don't see why not, so long as it's not about the case."

"I'd like to talk to you about the case," said Anne. "You really don't believe me, do you? I don't mean as a barrister cross-examining, but you as yourself don't believe me, do you?"

"I really can't discuss the case," said Coventry.

"Well, you think I'm a bad lot," said Anne, "don't you?"

"I think you're a singularly beautiful woman."

"Thank you. You may say that again."

"I shouldn't have said it once," said Coventry. "But everyone must know it."

"I said you were quite nice out of office hours," said Anne. "But you don't think I am, do you? You'd hate to know me, wouldn't you?"

"Well," said Coventry and hesitated. He was embarrassed by the cross-examination but almost enjoyed it. "Well," he repeated, "I'm a married man—"

"Don't married men talk to anyone except their wives, sisters, mothers, aunts, and other men? If things were different, would you like to take me out to lunch?"

At that moment Mrs. Coventry came in.

"Oh, I'm so sorry," she said. "I didn't know you were busy," and went out again.

"That was my wife," said Coventry.

"Charming," said Anne. "I don't somehow think she'd like me to lunch with you."

"I don't think any married woman would like her husband to lunch with you. You're far too attractive."

"Well, it won't happen, but it's nice to think about. Where would you take me?"

"I really don't know."

"Somewhere in town—or would we drive a little way out into the country?"

Coventry was now beginning to wish he hadn't been led into conversation.

"Is your car a comfortable one? Now I'm not discussing the case," she added quickly.

Coventry said nothing. He rather wished that his wife would return.

"I know a perfectly splendid little place about fifteen miles out—"

"This really won't do, Mrs. Preston," said Coventry. "We can't go on talking like this."

"What a shame," said Anne. "It's so much nicer than the other thing. And that's so one-sided. This way *I* can ask you questions."

"I'm afraid we must stop."

"Well, no hard feelings," said Anne.

"No," said Coventry.

"Well, I'm glad of that," said Anne. "And don't be too cross with me when I produce the letter."

"You've got it?"

"I'm afraid so. I told you you thought I was a liar."

"Well, I'm damned," said Coventry. "But I'm sorry," he added. "We mustn't talk about it."

"You couldn't help yourself," said Anne. "It took your breath away."

Outside the Court it would certainly have taken Jane's breath away. She was talking to Mr. Ringmer.

"I told Mr. Coventry she'd deny it," she said, "but I must confess I didn't think she'd have the cheek to say she'd got it."

"It's strange," said Mr. Ringmer.

"What's so strange?" said Jane. "She made a clever answer and had to get out of it somehow."

"Clever answer?"

"Yes, saying 'Would it surprise you if I produced the original?' when she'd already said she hadn't got it. Then she had to do something. So she pretended she'd got it after all. Don't you worry, Mr. Ringmer. She hasn't got it, for the very good reason that it doesn't exist and never has existed. And she can't forge it. She might manage the signature but she could never do the typewriter. No, she'll just come back with the sad story that she couldn't find it and she's so sorry."

"I expect you're right," said Mr. Ringmer.

"Expect!" said Jane indignantly. "I *am* right. If I never wrote such a letter, she can't have it, can she?"

"That's true," said Mr. Ringmer.

"Well, don't you believe that I never wrote it?"

"If you say you never wrote it," said Mr. Ringmer, "of course I accept it from you."

"You're all the same," said Jane. "You'd say the same to that bitch if you were appearing for her."

"Of course I should," said Mr. Ringmer. "We can only appear for one side or the other and it's our duty to do the best we can for whoever it is we appear for."

"But you don't have to believe them, do you?" said Jane.

"It's not for us to believe or disbelieve, but to do the best we can with the material we're given."

At that moment Anne passed them in the corridor. She did not look at either of them.

"Ah," said Jane. "I don't know what she's got in that bag but I can tell you what she hasn't."

It would certainly have taken Jane's breath away at that moment if she had seen Anne opening her bag and saying to Coventry:

"Like to have a look before the old judge gets back?"

"No," said Coventry firmly.

"Suppose I tell the judge you called me beautiful and attractive?" said Anne.

"You must tell him," said Coventry, "if you want to."

"Would he be angry?" asked Anne.

"He might be surprised, but I don't think he'd be angry."

"Suppose I said you'd invited me to lunch with you?"

"That wouldn't be true."

"Of course not, but suppose I said it?"

"I can't stop you saying anything," said Coventry, "but of course, if it isn't true, I shall deny it."

"And he'll believe you because you're you, I suppose."

"It doesn't matter what he believes. It's nothing to do with the case."

"It'd look funny in the newspapers."

Then seeing the look on Coventry's face she added quickly, "You don't think I'd really do that to you, do you? I think you're terribly sweet. I could fall for you in a big way. I'm not sure that I haven't."

Coventry remained silent, hoping that someone would come in. He felt it a little undignified to walk out.

"It's a pity about that car ride into the country," Anne went on. "Have you a central gear lever or is it on the steering?"

And then at last someone did come in. It was Tarrington. He was followed by the solicitors. Then came Mrs. Coventry. Shortly afterwards the usher returned with the judge. Anne returned to the witness box.

17 An Original Letter

"Now, Mrs. Preston," said Coventry, "have you managed to find the letter?"

"Yes, I have," said Anne.

"Will you produce it, please."

Anne handed the letter to the usher.

"Before it is handed to his lordship," said Coventry, "do you swear that this piece of paper is the actual letter you received from my client?"

"I swear it," said Anne.

"Would your lordship look at the letter first?" said Coventry.

The usher took the letter to the judge. He looked at it, readjusted his glasses, and looked at it carefully again. Then he handed it to the usher.

"Show this to counsel, please," he said. "You're in for a shock, Mr. Coventry."

The usher took the letter to Coventry, who beckoned to Tarrington to look at it with him.

"Good God!" said Coventry softly when he saw what it was. Then he said aloud to Anne, "Mrs. Preston, this letter is an exact copy of the one you said was a forgery, isn't it?"

"I know."

"But you swore the original said something quite different."

"I know."

"What is your explanation, madam?"

"I was mistaken. What I said must have been in the other letter I mentioned."

"But you said the copy was a forgery."

"I thought it was."

"But it isn't?"

"Obviously not."

"So my client did write and ask you to keep away from her husband?"

"Yes, she did."

"But you absolutely denied it."

"I can only swear to what I believe. I'd forgotten this letter."

"In spite of the striking nature of the language."

"Language means nothing to me. I'd treated it as nonsense from the start, and put it out of my mind."

"With extraordinary success."

"With unfortunate success."

"Are you asking his lordship to believe that there was another letter which says that, so long as you're serious, Mrs. Amberley doesn't mind the association?"

"I am."

"How on earth can the learned judge tell whether you're telling the truth or not?"

"Well, I needn't have brought this letter to court, need

I? I could just have said I couldn't find it and stuck to my story, couldn't I?"

"That's true, isn't it, Mr. Coventry?" said the judge.

"My lord, I hope that every time this witness is found out in a—in a misstatement, your lordship isn't going to say that it makes her more reliable than ever."

"I'm not going to say anything at the moment," said the judge.

At that stage Jane asked Mr. Ringmer to come outside.

"You see," she said as soon as they were in the corridor, "I did write the letter as I told you."

"You certainly did," said Mr. Ringmer.

"But you didn't believe me when I told you about it."

"Mrs. Amberley," said Mr. Ringmer. "I neither believed nor disbelieved you. We solicitors are not judges. How can I tell whether my client is telling me the truth? I may feel sure that he is and I may be wrong. I may feel sure that he isn't and I may be wrong."

"Well, that's what's happened this time," said Mrs. Amberley. "But I haven't brought you outside just to gloat. I want to assure you that this other letter she talks of is an absolute fabrication. I never thought it, I never wrote it, there is no truth in what she says at all."

"In view of what's happened, Mrs. Amberley," said Mr. Ringmer, "I believe what you say."

"Well, can you get Mr. Coventry to believe it? I want to win this case and, if my lawyers don't believe in me, what chance have I that the judge will? I'm sure judges can feel these things. Just like a woman can tell things which are never said. We sense them. I'm sure the judge can sense when a barrister doesn't believe in his client."

"Mr. Coventry is one of the ablest counsel at the bar, Mrs. Amberley, and—" began Mr. Ringmer.

"I know all that," said Jane. "You've told me so a hundred times. But if the judge knows the ablest counsel at the bar disbelieves in his client, what's the good of all the ability in the world? For two pins Mr. Coventry would have said that I'd forged that carbon copy. Well, now you've both seen. I'd genuinely mislaid it. But, if Mrs. Preston hadn't brought along the original, I don't believe either you or Mr. Coventry would have believed me for a moment."

"It's very odd that she should have brought it," said Mr. Ringmer. "I wonder why she did."

"She's got a reason all right," said Jane. "She's no fool. She wouldn't have brought it if it hadn't suited her."

"You may be right, but at the moment it only seems to harm her case. How could she really have forgotten a note in such dramatic language? How can the judge believe that she's telling the truth when she calmly says that language means nothing to her and that she'd put it out of her mind?"

"She's got something up her sleeve," said Jane. "She must have known that everyone would say she must have remembered it and that that would go against her."

"Perhaps she's gambling," said Mr. Ringmer. "Everything in this case depends on whether the judge is satisfied she's lying about the adultery. Perhaps she's thinking on these lines. How can a judge be sure that a witness is lying when she's voluntarily given such strong evidence against herself? He may disbelieve her on several matters, but would it be safe to convict her when she's proved that she can be exceptionally honest to her own disadvantage?"

"Well, she's up to something," said Jane. "There's no doubt about that. Now, when the Court adjourns, will you please have a word with Mr. Coventry and try to make him believe in me."

"Well, Mrs. Amberley, Mr. Coventry has a mind of his own and I can't make it up for him. But I shall be very surprised if the conclusive proof that you were right about the letter hasn't raised his opinion of you as a witness of truth very much indeed."

"How low was it before?" asked Jane.

At that moment Mrs. Coventry came out.

"Who's that?" whispered Jane to Mr. Ringmer.

"No idea," said Mr. Ringmer.

Without a word Jane left him and went after Mrs. Coventry.

"Excuse me," she said when she'd caught up with her.

"Yes?" said Mrs. Coventry.

"Forgive my asking," said Jane, "but I've noticed you in court and I wondered if you were anything to do with the case. I don't want to speak to you if you're a witness."

"No, I'm not a witness. I'm Mr. Coventry's wife as a matter of fact."

"Are you really?" said Jane. "Oh, I am glad I spoke to you. I should like to tell you how wonderful I think your husband is. I can't tell you how grateful I am to him."

"That's very good of you."

"Good of me? Not in the least. This case is terribly important to me. I've simply got to win it. I know I'm in the right. And your husband is doing wonders. I know it's not easy. They're such liars. I don't know how much you've heard."

"Only since this morning."

"Well, you've heard quite a bit then. What did you think of the letter? Pretty cool. Telling me I'd forged the copy and then producing the original."

"She's an extraordinary woman," said Mrs. Coventry. "I certainly wouldn't have wanted my husband to have been involved with her."

"And what a liar! Did you hear the way she said she'd never had a letter like that from me and then calmly brings it along? The judge can't believe that she'd forgotten all about it, can he?"

"Well, I wouldn't," said Mrs. Coventry.

"I'm so glad you agree. Do please tell your husband when you see him how much I admire him and how grateful I am for all he's doing."

"Thank you very much," said Mrs. Coventry. "I certainly will. I wish you the very best of luck. I'm sorry I can't stay to see the rest of it. But I have to get back home. Good-by and thank you for what you've said about my husband. I'm sure he'll be pleased."

Mrs. Coventry shook hands with Jane and went down the corridor. Jane went back to court. She arrived in time to hear Anne say:

"Well, Mr. Coventry, I'm a good deal more reliable than your inquiry agent."

"You've no right whatever to say that," said Coventry.

"Haven't I?" said Anne. "We'll see about that."

"What on earth are you talking about, Mrs. Preston?" asked the judge.

"You told me to bring my passport with me, my lord. Well, I have."

"What's that got to do with it?" said Coventry. "That's only to show when you went to the theater with Mr. Amberley. The inquiry agent said nothing about that."

"No, he didn't, did he?" said Anne and waited.

Mr. Ringmer began to sense that Anne really had a very high card to play; if not an ace, something very like it. But what could it be? Had she found out something against Mr. Brown? Convictions for perjury or something of that kind? But surely he'd have known of that. Jane had chosen Mr. Brown long before she consulted Mr. Ringmer. He would never have gone to a firm of that kind. But, though Mr. Brown was well known in the legal profession, Mr. Ringmer had certainly never heard that he'd been convicted. But, if it wasn't that, what could it be? Anne was still waiting, and, from the look on her face, it seemed pretty plain that on this occasion she was the angler and Coventry the fish.

"Well, Mrs. Preston," Coventry was eventually heard to say, "what is it you want to say about Mr. Brown?"

"I don't want to say anything about Mr. Brown," said Anne. "I merely said I was more reliable than he was. You said I had no right to say that and I said I had. That's all I want to say about Mr. Brown—directly."

"What d'you want to say about your passport then?" said Coventry.

"Oh, yes, my passport," said Anne. "It's a pity Mr. Brown didn't look at it when he broke into the flat. I'm sorry. Now I've said something about Mr. Brown again. As a matter of fact I was wrong to say I didn't want to criticize Mr. Brown. I do really."

"Madam," said the judge, "will you kindly come to the point. The witness box is not a place in which to enjoy yourself."

"Don't I know it, my lord," said Anne. "Look what happened to me earlier on."

"You appear to be enjoying yourself now, madam," said the judge. "And, if you go too far again, I may send you to prison instead of fining you. Courts of law are not meant to be places of entertainment for people to disport themselves in."

"I know, my lord," said Anne, "and I apologize for my behavior, but I've had a pretty grueling time here and I must admit that it's going to be a pleasant change to get a bit of my own back."

"Well, get it back, madam," said the judge, "but please don't take so much time over doing it. You are quite deliberately dragging out this particular episode in order to amuse yourself at someone else's expense. And I warn you for the last time that, if you go on any longer like this, it will most certainly be at your expense as well."

"Very well, my lord," said Anne, "I'll come straight to the point. Mr. Brown gave very definite evidence that on the evening of the 19th January Mr. Amberley came into my room at the hotel and stayed there for two hours late at night. He gave the most careful and detailed evidence about it. There was no room for mistake. He was either lying or telling the truth. Mr. Amberley and I both said it was untrue. It was suggested to both of us by Mr. Coventry that we were lying and that on the 19th January in that room in that hotel we slept together."

Anne paused for a moment. She obviously wanted to make the most of the situation without being dealt with for contempt of court.

"Well," she went on, "I'm prepared to admit that, if

Mr. Amberley and I were in that room in that hotel on the evening of the 19th January, we did commit adultery," she paused again. Then she opened her bag and brought out her passport. Mr. Ringmer guessed what was coming and he was right.

"My passport shows, my lord," Anne went on, "that I was not in England on the 19th January."

As she said that, Anne raised the passport and brought it down with a snap on to the edge of the witness box.

18 A Passport and Other Matters

"Let me see the passport," said the judge.

It was handed up to him and he looked at it carefully, turning over most of the pages before he said anything. Finally after about half a minute he spoke.

"She's quite right, Mr. Coventry, it does show that when she was supposed to be in Mr. Amberley's arms in the hotel she was not in England."

Anne looked triumphantly at Coventry.

Coventry whispered to Mr. Ringmer.

"Go and fetch Mr. Brown, please. We'll have to recall him. If he's got no explanation, that's an end of the case."

Amberley spoke to Tarrington.

"Doesn't that finish it?" he asked.

"I hope so," said Tarrington and got up.

"And this shows, my lord," he said, "that my client's ex-

planation of the entry in the diary is the correct one, and
that my learned friend's suggestion is wholly without foun-
dation."

"That seems to be right, Mr. Coventry, doesn't it?" said
the judge.

"Will your lordship give me a moment?" asked Coventry.

"You may have two," said the judge. "You may need
them."

Mr. Ringmer had not yet moved since Coventry had
asked him to fetch Mr. Brown.

"Do go and get Brown," said Coventry.

Mr. Ringmer went to the door and was about to open
it when the judge suddenly said loudly:

"Stop."

Mr. Ringmer remained rigid with one hand on the door
and one leg slightly raised as though he'd been suddenly
hypnotized and told by his control to remain in that position.

"No one is to leave this Court until I say so," said the
judge.

"Mr. Ringmer was going out at my suggestion to fetch
Mr. Brown," said Coventry. "I was proposing to ask your
lordship for leave to recall him before I continue my cross-
examination."

"That's what I thought," said the judge. "No one is to
speak to Mr. Brown before he is recalled except the usher."

"Mr. Ringmer wouldn't have said anything he shouldn't
to the witness," said Coventry.

"I accept that without qualification," said the judge,
"but in the circumstances you couldn't blame Mrs. Preston
or Mr. Amberley if they thought otherwise. It is very im-

portant that Mr. Brown should be absolutely unaware of what has happened before he comes back into the witness box. Usher, will you please bring in Mr. Brown."

The usher went out and called "Mr. Brown" loudly. He might have saved his breath as no one was in the corridor. He called again with the same result. He returned to the Court.

"No answer, my lord," he said.

"Then go and find him, please," said the judge. "He hasn't been told he can leave, I suppose."

"Most certainly not, my lord," said Coventry.

The usher went out again.

Tarrington leaned across to Coventry.

"What d'you think the odds are now?" he asked.

"I thought you weren't a betting man."

"I'm becoming one."

"Be warned in time," said Coventry. "It's winning the first time that starts the rot."

"Are you going to cave in then?" asked Tarrington.

"I'll see what Mr. Brown has to say first," said Coventry.

"Why isn't Mr. Brown back?" said the judge. "He ought to have stayed in the corridor. Look at the time wasted."

"I'm very sorry, my lord," said Coventry.

"It's the parties I'm thinking of," said the judge. "How much does this case cost a minute?"

"I've no idea, my lord."

"Well," said the judge, "it's as well that you and all the other lawyers connected with the case should have some idea. I'll work it out. It'll give me something to do."

"My lord," said Tarrington in a slightly offended tone, "my learned friend has asked for leave to recall Mr. Brown and Mr. Brown has been sent for, but your lordship hasn't asked me if I object to his being recalled."

"Don't interrupt, please," said the judge. "I'm working out the figures."

Let me see, he said to himself, assume the brief fees to be two hundred on each side. Refreshers would be, say, seventy-five a day. Juniors fifty. That's two hundred and fifty a day for refreshers. Allow the solicitors thirty a day each, that's sixty. Witness about ten of them, say thirty guineas. How much is all that? Two fifty and sixty is— It was at that stage that he said, "Don't interrupt, please," and had to start again. Two fifty and sixty is three hundred and ten and thirty is three hundred and forty. Say three-fifty. Five hours a day. Fives into three-fifty are seventy. Seventy pounds an hour. That's just over a pound a minute. "It works out at just over a pound a minute," he said aloud. "How many pounds has Mr. Brown cost by now?"

No one volunteered the information.

"It's too bad," said the judge. "Witnesses ought to remain in court or in the corridor outside."

"Your lordship hasn't yet dealt with my objection," said Tarrington.

"Well, what is your objection?" asked the judge. "It appears that Mr. Brown was telling lies or has made a bad mistake. Surely he must be given the opportunity of dealing with the matter."

"Certainly," said Tarrington, "if your lordship thinks that a man who breaks into other people's property should be given any latitude—"

"It isn't a question of giving anyone any latitude," interrupted the judge. "I want to find out the truth of the matter. Quite obviously Mr. Brown must be recalled."

"I'm not really opposing his being recalled," said Tarrington, "but why now? Why shouldn't the cross-examination of Mrs. Preston be completed first? Otherwise she'll be going in and out like a jack-in-the-box."

"Well, for one thing it gives her a rest," said the judge. "But, more important, this is a vital issue. If Mr. Brown can give no explanation, what's the point of going on with the case? At a pound a minute. And why should your client be subjected to further cross-examination? On the other hand, if there is an explanation, it's far more convenient to have it now."

"If your lordship pleases," said Tarrington.

"Well, where is the witness?" said the judge. "I think the solicitors on each side should go and help to find him. Will they please go together and stay together and say nothing to Mr. Brown except that he's wanted here at once."

Mr. Ringmer got up and went to the door and started to open it.

"Stop," said the judge.

Mr. Ringmer stopped but not quite as rigidly as before.

"Please wait till your colleague is with you. I thought I made it quite plain that I want you please to go *together* and stay together."

By this time the other solicitor had reached the door and they went out together.

"Almost feels as though I was back at school," said Mr. Ringmer to his colleague.

"It does a bit. The old boy's on the warpath all right."

They went out and, as soon as they were in the corridor, Mr. Ringmer suggested that they should go to the crypt. On the way there they passed the usher walking slowly and dolefully along the corridor, every now and then calling out

"Walter Brown." They suggested that he should go with them. In view of the judge's definite instructions they agreed that it would be best for the usher to speak to the witness.

"This is a very odd state of affairs," said Mr. Ringmer's opponent, a solicitor named Shuttle. "It looks as though we're going to get away with it."

"You don't seem to have much faith in your clients," said Mr. Ringmer.

"Not in one of my clients," commented Mr. Shuttle. "Amberley is as good a witness as I've had in cases of this kind but, between you and me, I wouldn't discharge the office boy on the word of the beautiful Anne."

"Have you got an office boy?"

"Well, we haven't as a matter of fact, but you know what I mean."

"But she seems to be right about this," said Mr. Ringmer. "Mark you," he added, "I wouldn't discharge anyone on the word of our Mr. Brown. So that takes two of them out. If they cancel out, that leaves only Amberley and you win easily. I agree with you about him. That's what's puzzled me for a long time."

"You're telling me," said Mr. Shuttle. "It's the oddest case I've ever had. And this last incident makes it even odder. I'll eat my hat if Mrs. Preston isn't a thorough-paced liar. Yet here she is trumping your ace with a vengeance. But I wonder why she didn't bring this out before."

That was what the judge was wondering and while Mr. Ringmer and Mr. Shuttle and the usher were searching for Mr. Brown he asked Anne some questions about it.

"Mrs. Preston," he said, "I see that you left London Airport on the 18th January and didn't return until several days later. So you were not in England on the 19th January."

"That is so, my lord."

"Mr. Brown said Mr. Amberley was in your room in the evening of that day."

"I said it was untrue."

"I know you did," said the judge, "but why did you wait till now to prove it was untrue?"

"Why did I wait till now?"

"Did you not hear the question, Mrs. Preston?"

"Yes, my lord."

"Then why repeat it?" said the judge. "What's the answer?"

"I'd forgotten. It was only when I looked in my passport to find the date I went to the theater that I . . ."

"How did you know we wanted that? You weren't in court when it was mentioned."

"The solicitor was on the phone when I got to the hotel, and he told me why the passport was wanted."

Tarrington got up.

"There was nothing wrong in that, I hope, my lord?" he said.

"No, nothing wrong, but it would have been better just to ask her to bring it. Go on, Mrs. Preston."

"So I looked at it," said Anne, "and then I saw the 18th January . . ."

"But you must have known all along that the date Mr. Brown mentioned was very close to the date you went abroad," said the judge.

"Yes, of course, my lord."

"Well, why didn't you look it up before?"

"I didn't see any point, my lord. I couldn't believe that

an inquiry agent would be such a fool as to choose a date when I wasn't there. I assumed that I must have been at the hotel and that all he invented was Mr. Amberley's visit."

"Well, when Mr. Brown comes we'll ask him."

"If he comes, my lord," said Tarrington.

"Are you suggesting he's disappeared?" said the judge.

"Not yet, my lord."

At that moment the door was thrown open and Mr. Brown rushed in. He was a small friendly-looking man, with gold spectacles. He had a red face. He talked rather fast and gave the impression (correctly as it happened) that he was anxious to please everyone. He was very much out of breath. He rushed into the witness box and stood panting and half-smiling.

"I'm sorry, my lord," he said, gasping.

"Get your breath back first," said the judge. "Where are the others?"

Mr. Brown pointed to the door.

"They're coming, my lord," he said. "They walked."

"Where were you?" asked the judge.

"I'm afraid I was having a beer, my lord."

"One?"

"At a time, my lord."

"You shouldn't have left the corridor."

"I didn't know I'd be wanted, my lord," said Mr. Brown.

"Well, now you do," said the judge. "Are you fit to give evidence? How many beers have you had?"

"Three or four, my lord. I met some friends."

"Well, are you fit?"

"Oh, yes, my lord. I've given evidence on much more than this."

"Oh, you have, have you? Well, don't do it again."

At that moment the usher came in, also gasping.

"He ran away, my lord . . ." he began. Then he saw Mr. Brown and added, "I'm sorry, my lord."

"That's all right," said the judge. "I should sit down if I were you." The usher sat down gratefully. A moment later Mr. Ringmer and Mr. Shuttle arrived, also very much out of breath. They went to their seats and sat down.

"Thank you, gentlemen," said the judge. "I'm sorry you've had so much trouble. Now, Mr. Brown," he went on, "are you ready? Would you like to sit down too?"

"No, thank you, my lord."

"He's your witness, Mr. Coventry. What would you like to ask him?"

"Mr. Brown," said Coventry, "you told us in your evidence that on the 19th January you concealed yourself near to Mrs. Preston's room in her hotel, and that you saw Mr. Amberley go in—and that he stayed there two hours late at night."

"That's right, my lord," said Mr. Brown. "I'm quite sure Mr. Amberley never saw me."

"The question is . . . did you see *him?*"

"Oh, yes, my lord. He was in a dressing gown and . . ."

"Just a moment, Mr. Brown," said Coventry.

"Now, no cross-examination, please," said Tarrington softly to Coventry.

"You can do it yourself if you like," whispered Coventry. "Yes—why not?" he added. Then, "I shall leave it to my learned friend," he said aloud and sat down.

Tarrington rose. "Now, Mr. Brown," he said, "you're quite sure what you've said is true?"

"Most certainly."

"Every word of it?"

"Well, I can't guarantee every comma . . ."

"Are you sober?" asked the judge.

"Oh, yes, my lord."

"Would it surprise you to learn," went on Tarrington, "that at the time you say Mr. Amberley was with Mrs. Preston she was several hundred miles away?"

"It would—very much." At that moment he saw the passport on the associate's desk. "Is that a passport?" he asked.

"Yes."

"Oh," said Mr. Brown.

"Why d'you ask? Does the sight of it upset you?" said Tarrington.

"It does a bit," said Mr. Brown.

"Perhaps you think you're seeing things?"

"I should like to think so," said Mr. Brown. "Of course it could be forged. Might I see it, my lord, please?"

"Show it to him," said the judge.

The passport was handed to Mr. Brown and he looked at it carefully. After a short time he said, "This is genuine all right. The fault must be mine."

"What fault, Mr. Brown?" asked Mr. Tarrington.

"Oh, come, sir, don't play with me. We all know what this is about . . ."

"Don't talk like that," said the judge.

"I'm sorry, my lord," said Mr. Brown and became silent.

"Go on," said the judge after a few seconds' silence.

"I'm frightened to," said Mr. Brown.

"No doubt," said Tarrington. "And why are you frightened?"

"His lordship's rebuke. It took the stuffing out of me."

"Don't talk like that," said the judge.

"You see?" said Mr. Brown.

"Mr. Brown," said the judge, "pull yourself together or I'll send you to prison."

Brown looked helplessly first at the judge and then at Tarrington.

"Go on, Mr. Tarrington," said the judge.

"You said the fault must be yours, Mr. Brown. What fault?"

"The date," said Mr. Brown. "I've got the date wrong. I've never done such a thing before. May I look in my diary, my lord?"

"Very well."

Brown got out his diary. As he started to look at it, he picked up the passport again.

"No, don't look at that again," said the judge.

"I don't want to give another wrong date, my lord."

"I dare say. Put that passport down. Mr. Associate, please put it on your desk."

The associate took the passport and put it on his desk.

"Well, Mr. Brown, what help have you got from your diary?"

After Mr. Brown had been looking at his diary for some little time, he frowned.

"Well," repeated Tarrington, "what help have you got from your diary?"

"None," said Mr. Brown, and then almost immediately he smiled and said, "Oh, yes, I have, my lord. It's quite plain now."

"What is quite plain?"

"I first of all copied out the entry from my diary and then I typed out what I'd copied. I must have mistaken 17 for 19. But you'll see it in my diary. It was all on the 17th."

"Let me see the diary and the passport," said the judge.

The usher took the diary from Mr. Brown and gave it to the associate, who handed both to the judge.

"We've never seen this diary before," said Tarrington. "We were told it was lost."

"That's quite right, my lord," said Mr. Brown. "I thought I'd lost it when I moved offices. Only found it last night. Lucky."

Meanwhile the judge had been looking at the diary and the passport.

"Mrs. Preston," he said, "were you in England on the 17th of January?"

"Yes, my lord."

"Staying at the hotel?"

"Yes, my lord."

"And not registered?"

"I've explained that."

"Back to square one," whispered Coventry to Tarrington.

"This diary looks genuine enough," said the judge. "Anything more you want to ask Mr. Brown, Mr. Tarrington?"

"Not at the moment, my lord."

"Mr. Coventry?"

"No, thank you, my lord."

"May I go back, please, my lord?" said Mr. Brown.

"You may not. You will stay in court."

"May I go out for a few minutes, my lord?"

"Certainly not."

"It's rather awkward, my lord."

"I dare say it is. You should have thought of that before."

"But, my lord . . ."

"If you want to go to a convenience, the usher shall go with you and come back with you."

"It's not that, my lord, but I haven't paid for the last round."

"It can wait. You sit down there, and stay there till I adjourn."

Mr. Ringmer felt much relieved. He was quite used to losing a case which he had hoped to win and he accepted such defeats philosophically and went on with the next case. But, having convinced himself that Anne was lying and that, therefore, Amberley was too, he had been very much shocked to find that apparently not merely was Mr. Brown a liar but that he could be conclusively proved to be one. But the explanation of the mistake about the date sounded genuine and seemed to be accepted by the judge. It also accounted for the fact that Anne had only taken the point at a very late stage. This reinforced Mr. Ringmer's view that she and Amberley had been together in the room as Mr. Brown had said. If the thing had been purely imaginary and Anne had not ever been in the hotel, surely she would have referred to the matter earlier in her evidence. The judge had obviously thought on the same lines and, now that it appeared that there was simply a mistake in the date, it convinced Mr. Ringmer that the petitioner's allegations were correct.

Coventry then got up.

"In view of that evidence, my lord," he said, "I ask for leave to amend the date in paragraph eleven of the petition to the 17th of January."

"What do you say, Mr. Tarrington?"

"I object," he said. "Normally of course I wouldn't object to a date being changed by two days. But this case is quite exceptional. It has been said that there has been a mistake. For the purposes of my argument I'm prepared to assume that there has been a mistake, but who made it? Mr. Brown, the man who has not scrupled to use what your lordship describes as the most deplorable methods to obtain evidence. Your lordship has allowed the evidence secured in this outrageous manner to be used to support my learned friend's case. Your lordship has said that that was not a matter of discretion but that as a matter of law my friend is entitled to rely on the evidence, however obtained. Very well, my lord, so be it. But now my learned friend is asking for latitude. He is asking you to exercise your discretion in his favor and give him leave to amend. Why should latitude be shown to a petitioner who, through her agent—Mr. Brown—conducts her case in such a manner? What she is entitled to in law, that she must have. But why more? Particularly when it is the very agent of whom I complain who has made the mistake. I ask your lordship to refuse to give my learned friend leave to amend."

"What do you say, Mr. Coventry?" asked the judge. "Why should I assist your client in the circumstances?"

"Because the justice of the case requires it, my lord," said Coventry. "First of all, the petitioner is Mrs. Amberley and not Mr. Brown. Secondly, neither Mrs. Amberley nor Mrs. Preston will be prejudiced in any way by the amendment. It is little more than a formal amendment. Indeed if the petition had said 'On or about the 19th January' instead of 'On the 19th January,' no amendment would have been necessary. As your lordship knows, although leave to amend is discretionary, the rules provide that all such amendments necessary to determine the real question in controversy between the parties *shall* be made, not *may* but *shall*. Mr. Brown's behavior over the letter and the diary has nothing whatever to do with the alteration of the date. The explanation for the wrong date has been given. It was purely an accident, and it would be grossly unjust if the respondents succeeded on the purely technical point that the 19th had been put in the petition instead of the 17th. Moreover, it would really serve no useful purpose, for, if the petitioner failed in these proceedings simply on the ground that the 17th had not been pleaded, a further petition could be launched in which that allegation of adultery could be made. No one wants this case tried all over again."

"Mr. Tarrington," said the judge, "on consideration I don't think it makes much difference whether I give leave to amend or not. There are three allegations of adultery. If I disbelieve Mr. Brown about the car incident, it will be unlikely that I shall believe him about the 19th January. Conversely, if I believe him about the car incident, the petitioner is entitled to a decree whether the incident on the 17th January is proved or not. In these circumstances I don't think leave to amend will do your client any injustice, and in these circumstances I shall give leave, unless you have anything to add."

"If your lordship pleases," said Tarrington and sat down.

"Very well," said the judge. "Now let's get on with the evidence. Have you more to ask Mrs. Preston, Mr. Coventry?"

"I'm afraid so, my lord."

"Please come back into the witness box, Mrs. Preston," said the judge.

Anne walked back to the witness box and sat down. As she sat down she sighed slightly.

"I'm sorry about this, Mrs. Preston," said Coventry.

"You have your duty to do," said Anne.

"I'm glad you appreciate that," said Coventry.

"Of course I do," said Anne.

"Thank you," said Coventry.

"When you two have finished chatting to one another," said the judge, "we might get on with the case."

"I'm sorry, my lord," said Coventry, "but I wanted the witness to know that I really am sorry for the ordeal she has to go through."

"If you're as sorry as all that," said the judge, "you should give up the bar. We all have to do many distasteful things in the administration of justice."

"I cannot accept your lordship's rebuke," said Coventry. "It is right for counsel to let witnesses know from time to time that they appreciate and sympathize with their position even though they have to cross-examine them severely. I'm afraid, therefore, my lord, I cannot apologize for my remarks to Mrs. Preston."

"It's my fault really," said Anne.

"Don't you start too," said the judge. "Mr. Coventry in his new role of Sir Galahad is bad enough."

This reference made Coventry think for a moment of the picture of the knight with eyes averted rescuing the naked lady, and he wondered what Anne would look like without her clothes. But he soon recovered. He had to win this case and Anne was by no means defeated yet.

"Mrs. Preston," he began, "I'd like there to be no doubt about this. You have, I know, sworn generally that you have never committed adultery with Mr. Amberley, but do you swear that he did not come to your room on the 17th January?"

"Not on that day or on any other—while I was there," said Anne.

"What did you do on the 17th January?" asked Coventry.

"Oh, really," said Anne, "how on earth do I know?"

"Would your diary help you?"

"I doubt it but I'll look—if you'll be kind enough to hand me my own property."

The diary was handed to Anne.

"Can I keep this now, my lord?" she asked the judge.

"Certainly," he said, "subject only to the Court's having it when it's required. At the moment it's an exhibit in the case and is therefore in the custody of the Court. But I shall make it plain that, when it is no longer required by the Court, it is to be handed over to no one except you or your solicitor."

"Thank you, my lord."

Anne looked at the diary. The entry for the 17th was blank.

"It doesn't help," she said.

"But how did you spend your days in the hotel generally?" asked Conventry.

"Much the same as you would, I suppose," said Anne.

"I'm afraid people vary," said Coventry. "I always make for the nearest golf course and spend most of my time there."

"I can't stand the game," said Anne. "Hitting a little ball—"

"Mrs. Preston," warned the judge, "be careful. I don't want to have to fine you again."

"I'm sorry, my lord. Well, I suppose I ate and drank and went for a walk or two, chatted with people. I really don't know what I did do on any particular day. I went for a swim in the river early one morning. With nothing on," she added. "But I was alone and no one could see except a cow or two."

"What time did you go to bed?"

"On that night?"

"If you can tell me."

"I can't. I suppose if you showed me the TV program for that night I might remember that I saw something in the TV lounge, which would mean that I couldn't have gone to bed before a particular time."

"Did you talk much to Mr. Amberley?"

"I expect so."

"Where?"

"In one of the public rooms. The bar or the lounge probably, unless, as I say, we wanted to see something on TV."

"Who went to bed first?"

"I've no idea."

"Is it possible that you went at the same time?"

"Of course it's possible."

"Did he see you to your room?"

"What do you mean by that?"

"What I say. Did he take you to your room?"

"If we went up together, my room was on the way to his, he will have walked with me till I came to my room. Then he would have gone upstairs and I would have gone into my room."

"Leaving it open?"

"Certainly. I hardly ever lock it. And it's easier for the

maid bringing the tea in the morning if she hasn't to use a key."

"Did Mr. Amberley ever bathe in the river?"

"I never saw him. He may have."

"Never with you?"

"I went only once. He certainly wasn't there on that occasion to my knowledge."

"He could have been spying from behind a hedge."

"So might you," said Anne, "but I don't suppose you were."

"How much of you has Mr. Amberley ever seen?"

"What on earth d'you mean by that?" asked Anne.

"It's certainly an ambiguous question," said the judge. "You should make it quite plain what you are asking, Mr. Coventry."

"I will, my lord. Has he ever seen you otherwise than fully dressed?"

"Certainly not."

"Are you quite sure of that?"

"Of course I am."

"I want there to be no doubt about this," said Coventry, "you see—"

"There is no doubt whatever," interrupted Anne.

"Please let me finish. You have made one or two mistakes in this case already. I don't want you to give me an answer now and later on tell me that it was a mistake. Had you a private bathroom?"

"No."

"So that when you wanted to use the bathroom or lavatory you had to leave your room."

"Yes."

"Usually, of course, when that sort of thing happens people put on dressing gowns. But occasionally it happens that the bathroom is so close or the person concerned in such a hurry that people in their underclothes with a dressing gown over their arms dash from the bathroom to their bedroom or vice versa. It doesn't happen often but it does occasionally happen."

"I'll take your word for it," said Anne. "You obviously notice such things more than I do. Anyway I can't speak for other people, only for myself. And I can say that I always wear a dressing gown."

"So that in no circumstances can Mr. Amberley ever have seen you anywhere in your underclothes?"

"No, he has not."

"It's no use my asking you whether that is as true as the rest of your evidence," said Coventry, "because his lordship doesn't approve of the question."

"Then why on earth say anything about it?" said the judge.

"I thought that possibly in the special circumstances of this case your lordship might not think it so unreasonable a question."

"Earlier on I described it as a footling question. I see no reason to change my opinion," said the judge.

"Earlier on," said Coventry, "I respectfully complained at your lordship's use of such an adjective and I complain again. Your lordship then invited me to omit the respect. So I simply complain."

"Don't waste time, please," said the judge.

The judge won on the exchange, but it is only on comparatively rare occasions that he does not. The scales are so heavily weighted in his favor. If he cannot think of a satisfactory answer he can simply say nothing. Silence by itself is often a very effective weapon. Judge Brace was not, however, a judge who abused his power. He had no wish to score off Coventry. He objected to the particular line of questioning and said so. When Coventry sought to complain about this in rather lengthy terms, he was in fact wasting time, and so the judge asked him not to.

"Now, Mrs. Preston," said Coventry, "you know, do you not, that, while you were fetching the letter and the passport, Mr. Amberley gave further evidence?"

"So I've heard," said Anne.

"Do you also remember saying that, when you and he were alone in court and we came and interrupted you, you were saying it was lucky that we didn't hear what you said about me?"

"Something like that."

"Mr. Amberley has told us that what you were saying, when we interrupted you, was that it was lucky we didn't know about . . . and then came the interruption."

"He said that?"

"He did. Is that what you in fact said?"

"I'm sure I wouldn't have said a thing like that."

"He says you did."

"What did he say I was referring to?"

"He said he couldn't for the life of him think what you meant. He said he thought about the matter for some time, but he couldn't think what it was. It sounds as though you said it, doesn't it?"

"Yes, it does. I suppose I must have said it."

"Well, think again, please. What was it it was lucky we didn't know about you and Mr. Amberley?"

"I've no idea."

"Now look, Mrs. Preston," said Coventry, "this episode took place only a short time ago. I suggest to you that, if you said 'It's lucky they didn't know about something,' it is quite impossible that you should now have forgotten what that something was."

"I can't stop you making suggestions," said Anne.

"I'm not going to be put off as easily as that," said Coventry. "Do you positively swear that you have absolutely no idea of the subject to which you can have been referring?"

Anne did not answer immediately. Then:

"You're quite right, Mr. Coventry," she said. "I ought to know what I was referring to. Let me think."

"But surely, madam," said Coventry, "you don't have to think in order to remember something so recent."

"You've obviously never been a witness, Mr. Coventry," said Anne. "You have to think all the time. I'm being cross-examined minutely about all sorts of things by a very professional advocate. If I don't think I may make a silly answer or at any rate an answer which gives you material for more questions."

"Mrs. Preston," said the judge, "all a witness is required to do is to answer the truth to the best of his or her ability."

"That sounds easy, my lord," said Anne, "but I wish some of you lawyers were sometimes at the receiving end. I intend no impertinence, my lord, but it's often difficult enough in ordinary conversation to remember something that's only happened very recently. I'm surprised that in the witness box I can remember anything at all. My whole reputation is at stake. I've got to think of my answers. Think of the very first question I was asked. Why didn't I commit adultery with Mr. Amberley? Surely one has got to think before answering such a question. Then I'm asked sometimes about things that have happened in this Court and sometimes about things which happened years and years ago. It's easy for counsel to jump from one thing to another. He's got everything written down. He's ready for it all. I'm not. The only thing I came here to say was that I hadn't slept with Michael—"

"Michael?" interrupted Coventry, emphasizing Anne's use of the Christian name.

"His name's Michael and I used to call him Michael. But there you are, my lord. That's quite a good example of what I mean. I accidentally call Mr. Amberley Michael in the witness box. I call him Michael in the normal way, but because I say 'Michael' in the witness box I'm jumped on by Mr. Coventry. I suppose the suggestion is that, because I called him Michael in this Court, I slept with him."

"Well," said the judge, "that would be a pretty stupid suggestion."

"Thank you, my lord," said Anne. "But why else did Mr. Coventry intervene? If that wasn't the suggestion, what was the object of the interruption? Anyway, whatever the object, it shows how terribly careful I have to be in choosing every word. And then I'm asked why I have to think."

"All right, Mrs. Preston," said Coventry. "Think. Think as long as you like within reason, and when you've thought, tell his lordship what it was that it was lucky for you and Mr. Amberley that we didn't know."

"All right," said Anne, "I'll try."

After about ten or fifteen seconds she suddenly smiled.

"Of course," she said. "I remember now. If you think it's extraordinary that I shouldn't have remembered before,

I absolutely agree. But that's what happens here. One's so tensed up waiting for the next blow that one's mind is in a whirl."

"Well, as you've thought of it now," said Coventry, "perhaps you'd tell us."

"It was simply this. I once went to Mr. Amberley's room but apparently your Mr. Brown was in the bar at the time. At any rate he never saw us. But what a lot he could have made of it. I was there for three minutes. But he would have made it thirty. And by the time it had got into your hands, Mr. Coventry, he would have seen unmentionable things through the keyhole. And there'd have been another paragraph to this petition, and, unless he made another mistake in extracting the entry from his diary, I shouldn't have been able to prove that I was in Geneva at the time."

"When did you go to his room?"

"I couldn't possibly tell you the date."

"What did you go for?"

"I'm not even sure of that. May have been to fetch him to go for a walk. May have been to borrow something or to return something I'd borrowed. I simply don't know. I simply know that I did go there. Possibly it was to say I couldn't meet him or something. And I was there for three whole minutes. No, I didn't time it. Could I swear it wasn't more? No, I couldn't. It certainly wasn't as much as ten minutes. That's all I'd swear to. And the door was open all the time."

"If this is correct," said Coventry, "why is it lucky that we never heard about it?"

"Oh, really, Mr. Coventry," said Anne, "you're not serious."

"Of course, I'm serious. Why was it lucky we didn't know about it?"

"I've already told you," said Anne. "Because your inquiry agent would have distorted the incident in the way that I've suggested. It's always more effective for a lie to have some kind of basis. If we were in the room together, we couldn't deny it. All Mr. Brown has to do is to close the door and exaggerate the time. And, if looking through the keyhole is too difficult, he could say he heard our conversation. Oh, I could write his evidence for him, all right."

"What time of day was this?"

"If I say it was midday you'll say that I'm saying that because I've a guilty conscience."

"Mrs. Preston," said the judge, "don't do it. What time of day was it?"

"About six in the evening. Oh, yes. I remember now. I'd been going to dine with him in the hotel, and then I had a phone call and had to go up to town. So I went to tell him I couldn't make it. That's it. And I'll tell you another thing. If your snooper had been listening he'd have heard him say that I looked lovely in the dress I was wearing or something of the sort."

"And what did you say?"

"Probably 'Thank you, sir.' That's my usual reply to compliments."

"Can you remember any other part of the conversation?" asked Coventry.

"May I think again?" asked Anne.

"Certainly," said Coventry.

"I believe it's coming back to me," said Anne. "Wait a minute."

"Yes," she said after about half a minute. "I've got quite a bit for you. You'll like it."

"Mrs. Preston," said the judge. "I don't at the moment know whether you're making up your evidence as you go along or whether it's true. But I do know that you appear to be trying to amuse yourself. I've already fined you and I've warned you several times since then. I should very much dislike sending you to prison for playing the fool. But the courts couldn't be carried on unless reasonable order were maintained. I've given you a lot of latitude because I do realize, as it happens, that giving evidence must be a very great strain, particularly when the issue is a serious one. And I also realize that one method of trying to combat the strain is by an appearance of frivolity, and that that is the method you have sometimes adopted. But I cannot allow any more. If you continue to play about, I shall very regretfully have to send you to prison."

Anne's answer was to burst into tears.

"Mrs. Preston," said the judge, "I am also aware that that is another method adopted by witnesses. The waterworks do not impress me. Kindly dry your eyes and continue with your evidence."

Anne sniffed several times, blew her nose, and stopped crying.

"I'm afraid I've forgotten where I was," she said.

"You were going to tell me what was said between you and Mr. Amberley when you went to his room," said Coventry gently.

Anne rewarded his gentleness with a smile.

"Well," she said, "on that occasion Mr. Amberley did say something like 'If I weren't married, I believe I could fall for you quite easily.'"

"And what did you say?"

"Probably 'Thank you, sir.' "

"Is that all?"

"As far as I remember. I didn't take it very seriously. And even if he meant it, I knew there was no point in taking it seriously. His marriage meant a lot to him."

"Did he kiss you on that occasion?"

Anne hesitated.

"Why do you hesitate?"

"Well, I've got to be very careful about this. I've already come to grief over kisses. I really must think."

She waited several seconds before saying:

"No, he didn't. Quite definitely he didn't."

"Why do you say that with such emphasis?"

"Because I happen to remember. The truth is that I rather expected that he would, but he didn't."

"D'you find it easier to remember occasions when you weren't kissed than when you were?" asked Coventry.

"Perhaps," said Anne. "Certainly it makes an impression if you're expecting to be kissed and aren't."

"Were you disappointed?"

"I expect so. After all, it's a compliment. And I liked him too."

"And that's all that happened on that occasion?"

"To the best of my recollection."

At that stage Mr. Shuttle whispered to Amberley:

"What do you say about this?"

"It's about right," said Amberley. "And I didn't kiss her. I was going to and changed my mind."

"Why?" whispered Mr. Shuttle.

"I think because we were in my bedroom. I realized it would be dangerous and might lead to other things."

"If you want to take instruction at length from your client," said the judge, "please go outside. I don't mind the odd word or two but it's distracting to have lengthy conversations carried on while I'm listening to something else."

"Is there by chance anything else," continued Coventry, "which it's lucky we don't know of?"

"Dozen of things, I expect," said Anne.

"Dozens of things?" queried Coventry.

"What I mean is that every innocent action of every innocent person can by distortion, exaggeration, or even sometimes by omissions be made to appear a crime by unscrupulous investigators like Mr. Brown."

"You have nothing more specific in mind than that? No other incidents like your visiting Mr. Amberley in his room?"

"Certainly not."

"How can you be so sure when you'd forgotten about that incident until a few minutes ago?"

"I'm beginning to think I can't be sure of anything. You're perfectly right. That incident may be important to you but I'd forgotten it because it wasn't important to us. So there may be other incidents that might be important to you but I've forgotten because they weren't important to us. I can only assure you that anything that I have forgotten could only in fact be important in this case if it were grossly altered or distorted or exaggerated."

"But take this incident in Mr. Amberley's bedroom. You say it's innocent. But it isn't normal, is it, for you to go into a man's bedroom in a hotel? Even with the door open."

"No, I can't actually recall another occasion. But quite likely there was one, but I can't remember it as I've attached no importance to it. After all, it wouldn't be such a terrible thing these days just to go into a man's room in the day. One might be playing tennis or anything and have gone to fetch him. It must happen hundreds of times."

"No doubt," said Coventry, "but it's rather bad luck that it should have happened to you, who have suffered so many misfortunes."

"What on earth d'you mean?" said Anne.

"What Mr. Coventry means," said the judge, "is that it is another coincidence. He's really addressing me, not questioning you, and he shouldn't, until the time comes."

At that moment a man came into court and went and whispered to Mr. Brown. Mr. Brown whispered to Mr. Ringmer and Mr. Ringmer then indicated to Coventry that he wanted to speak to him.

"Would your lordship forgive me a moment?" said Coventry.

Mr. Ringmer informed Coventry that Mr. Brown had something important to say to him but that he couldn't go outside without the judge's permission.

"My lord," said Coventry, "Mr. Brown is remaining in court on your lordship's orders. My client would like to take some instructions from him. May he go outside for that purpose? He will, of course, return immediately afterwards."

"Certainly," said the judge.

Mr. Ringmer, Mr. Brown, and the man who had just arrived went outside.

"Thumbs up," said Mr. Brown.

"What is it?" said Mr. Ringmer.

"We've really got it this time," said Mr. Brown. "This is my colleague Mr. Moriarty."

"Pleased to meet you," said Moriarty.

"Well, what is it?" said Mr. Ringmer.

"We shall all be able to go home in a few minutes," said Mr. Brown.

"Mr. Brown," said Mr. Ringmer, "you may or may not be an excellent inquiry agent but you have the most provoking and irritating habit of not giving the result of your inquiries until one has asked you several times. It's very aggravating."

"Don't I know it?" said Mr. Brown. "You're not the first party who's complained about it. Not by a long chalk. Most people don't like roundabouts. They want it all straight and cut and dried. No beating about the bush, no preliminaries, out with it and be done."

"Those are my views exactly," said Mr. Ringmer.

"I thought they were," said Mr. Brown, "and, if I may say so, without meaning any disrespect, they're a credit to you. I don't mind telling you that if I were in your position I should feel exactly the same. Cut the cackle, I should say, and come to the 'osses."

"How right you are, Mr. Brown," said Moriarty. "How very right."

"But you see, Mr. Ringmer," went on Mr. Brown, "we have to have our perks like everyone else. And beating about the bush is one of mine. I like it. If I didn't allow myself that bit of fun I should have to charge more for my services, and go to the pictures with the extra. Now, Mr. Ringmer, you *could* say to me, 'All right, if you won't tell me, you won't' and walk off in a huff. But you can't really. You've a duty to your client. Of course if you thought I was just bluffing, that would be one thing. But you know that when I say I've got something I have got something.

Remember last time. Not as good as it might have been but pretty good all the same. But this is a cinch. This'll make your hair curl like the judge's wig—and Mr. Coventry's. Come to think of it, he's got more curls on his wig than the judge. Wonder why that is. You wouldn't know, I suppose?"

"No, I would not," said Mr. Ringmer angrily. "Are you going to tell me or aren't you?"

"There you go," said Mr. Brown. "Just as I said. But you won't walk off in a huff because you know you'd be letting down your client if you did. And, of course, she might sue you for negligence. Have you ever been sued for negligence, Mr. Ringmer?"

"I have not," said Mr. Ringmer quickly and icily.

"Good," said Mr. Brown. "Nor have I. That's another thing we have in common."

Mr. Ringmer said nothing. Mr. Brown was quite right. He felt sure that Mr. Brown had something of use to tell him, and he must just wait until he was prepared to tell him. But it was infuriating. He would never employ Mr. Brown again anyway.

"Mr. Brown," he said eventually, "Mr. Coventry may be coming to the end of his cross-examination. If this is material you have for cross-examining Mrs. Preston and you don't let me have it at once, it may be too late."

"Ah," said Mr. Brown. "That's clever. Clever that is. And if he missed the boat because of me having my perks I might be sued for negligence. Fair enough. I like an opponent worthy of my steel. Right. Mr. Moriarty, will you kindly put your hand in your right coat pocket and produce the rabbit."

Moriarty brought out an envelope.

"I'm glad to tell you, Mr. Ringmer, that we've got the photograph."

"You've got it?" said Mr. Ringmer quite excitedly. He was referring to a photograph of Anne in her underclothes sitting on a bed. Mr. Brown had informed Mr. Ringmer earlier on that such a photograph had been found in Amberley's room which Moriarty had visited. But most unfortunately the photograph had been mislaid. Coventry had waited as long as he could before cross-examining about it, in the hope that it would turn up in time. Mr. Ringmer was quite right in warning Mr. Brown that, if he didn't give his information soon, it might be too late. In fact while they were talking outside Coventry had been cross-examining Anne on the subject.

"Tell me, Mrs. Preston," he said, "was there nothing else you thought it was lucky we didn't know about except this visit to Mr. Amberley's room."

"Nothing," said Anne.

"You weren't by any chance worried about a photograph, were you?"

"What did you say?" said Anne, apparently a little disturbed.

"About a photograph."

"What about a photograph?"

"You tell me," said Coventry.

"I've nothing to tell. Have you some sort of a photograph?"

"Don't be so impatient, Mrs. Preston," said Coventry. "Were you worried that we might know something about a photograph?"

"Of course not. And I don't know what you mean by being worried. Why should I be?"

"Why, indeed—if we haven't got it."

"Oh, I see," said Anne. "Some kind of stupid bluff, I suppose."

"By all means call it that."

Tarrington rose.

"By no manner of means call it that," he said. "My lord, I've complained about this cross-examination more than once, but this really is beyond anything. My learned friend is deliberately trying to trick my client into thinking he has some compromising photograph of her when he hasn't anything of the sort. I ask your lordship to refuse to allow any further cross-examination of Mrs. Preston."

"Mr. Tarrington," said the judge, "you and I have known Mr. Coventry for many years. I'm quite sure that he would never do anything improper. Aren't you?"

"Really, my lord, I don't know what to say," said Tarrington. "It reminds me of a cross-examination in the United States where a lawyer got admissions out of a witness by pretending that he had in his hand some vital documents, when in fact what he held was blank paper."

"Well," said the judge, "at any rate justice was done as a result."

"Justice might be done," replied Tarrington, "by holding a witness's head in a bath full of water until he admitted the truth, but it's not our way of arriving at it. We prefer a bit of injustice now and then to those methods."

"That's true, Mr. Tarrington," said the judge. "But, I repeat, don't you trust your learned opponent?"

"Well, of course, in the normal way I would. But my client has been cross-examined for hours like a pickpocket, my learned friend has raked up the past—thirteen years of it—he's sneered at her—your lordship may remember reproving him for that—and now he's trying to pretend he's got something up his sleeve in order to make her nervous. Who wouldn't be nervous in the circumstances? Your lordship may be different, but I'd hate to think of anyone going through all my life with a microscope."

"Thank you for saying I might be different," said the judge. "I think Mr. Coventry had better continue."

"Thank you, my lord," said Coventry. "Mrs. Preston, is there a photograph which you're frightened might get into our hands?"

"Certainly not."

"We shall see," said Coventry.

"What does that mean?" said the judge.

"What I say. We shall see."

"I don't like that sort of comment by counsel. When counsel gets an answer he doesn't want, he's no business to say 'We shall see' in order to cover up his disappointment."

"I wasn't disappointed, my lord," said Coventry. "For once I really did mean what I said. We shall see."

"Well, you've no business to have said it."

"With respect, we shall see."

"Mr. Coventry, behave yourself," said the judge.

"I am, my lord. I'm perfectly entitled to suggest—with respect—that your lordship is wrong."

"I've said before—you can leave out the respect."

"Surely, my lord, the courtesies in court as well as in life are worth preserving."

"Get on with your cross-examination," said the judge.

"Very well, then, my lord. Mrs. Preston, I'm sure you appreciate that my client wouldn't instruct me to make allegations against you unless she thought they were justified."

"I appreciate no such thing," said Anne. "It's your client who's hounding me through the witness box. She has to do it through you, but the questions are hers—not yours. Even though she loses the case, as she will, she'll have the satisfaction of knowing that I've been through hell."

"If she takes such a delight in torturing you, Mrs. Preston," said Coventry, "can you think why it is that she chose to go out of the Court, instead of remaining here to gloat?"

"I certainly can. She was afraid that her obvious malice might show in her face as she sat there, and be observed by the judge."

"Well, she's wasting her time then," said the judge. "I never take any notice of how people look when they're sitting in court."

"She was not to know that, my lord," said Anne.

"That is all I wish to ask for the moment, my lord," said Coventry.

"For the moment!" said Tarrington. "How many more times has my client got to go backwards and forwards into the witness box?"

"Only once, I should think."

"Doesn't that rest with me?" said the judge.

"Of course, my lord."

"I just wanted to be sure," said the judge. "You may leave the box, Mrs. Preston."

19 A Photograph

Anne stepped down from the box and Tarrington rose.

"My lord," he said, "could Mr. Brown be recalled from outside the Court? I should like to ask him a few more questions."

"Certainly," said the judge. "Call him, usher."

The usher went out.

"Mr. Brown, you're wanted," he said.

Mr. Brown left Mr. Ringmer and Moriarty with the photograph and hurried in. Mr. Ringmer and Moriarty followed.

"Come back to the box, please, Mr. Brown," said Tarrington.

Mr. Brown hurried into the witness box.

"You understand that you're still on oath," said Tarrington.

"Quite so. Absolutely. Of course," said Mr. Brown.

"Now, Mr. Brown, someone broke into Mrs. Preston's flat in London and took some documents. Was it you?"

"I'm afraid so. May I apologize?"

"D'you often do that sort of thing?"

"Whenever it's necessary."

"Have you no respect for other people's property?"

"Of course I have."

"You have? Then how d'you come to do this sort of thing?"

"Quite simple, sir. My desire for the information outweighs my respect."

"Do you realize that if you were caught breaking in you might be mistaken for a burglar?"

"Of course. I have been."

"And charged?"

"Once."

"What happened?"

"I was acquitted, of course."

"You aren't a burglar in your spare time, I suppose?"

"What a horrible suggestion. Certainly not. I only take things to do with a case, and they're all handed back at the end. No *animus furandi*, you see, if you'll forgive the expression."

At that moment Anne asked Tarrington to put a question to Mr. Brown.

"Mr. Brown," said Tarrington after he had received Anne's instructions, "did you break into Mr. Amberley's room as well as Mrs. Preston's?"

"Did I break into Mr. Amberley's room? The answer is 'No.' I couldn't get the passkey."

"So you would have?"

"Of course. That's what I'm paid for."

"You mean Mrs. Amberley told you to break into my client's premises?"

"She told me to get the evidence."

"By fair means or foul?"

"If that's how you like to put it."

"How would you put it?"

"How would I put it? Yours will do very well. By fair means or foul."

"And do you ask his lordship to believe what you say?"

"Of course not," said Mr. Brown. "I leave it to him—unaided."

"How many private dwellings have you broken into?"

"How many? I couldn't possibly say."

"A hundred?"

"A hundred? I'd have to think. I'm fifty-three, and I've been doing this for nine years."

"What were you before?" asked the judge.

"A window cleaner, my lord," said Mr. Brown. "Now, let me think. Nine years—a hundred . . . that would be about one a month. No, not so many."

"Aren't you ashamed of yourself?" asked Tarrington.

"Ashamed of myself? Sometimes."

"When?"

"When? When I lose a case."

"You'd do anything to win your case, wouldn't you?"

"Not anything, but a good deal."

"Including telling lies?"

"Oh, no. Not that."

"Conscience?"

"Dear me, no. I don't tell lies, because the truth has a nasty habit of coming out."

"Has it come out in this case yet, do you think?"

"I've not been in court all the time, my lord."

"Quite so," said the judge.

"That's all I want to ask."

At that stage Mr. Ringmer told Coventry the latest news.

"May I have Mrs. Preston back now, my lord?" said Coventry. The judge nodded assent and Anne went back into the witness box.

"I knew this would happen," said Tarrington.

"It'll be the last time—I think," said Coventry.

"We shall see," said Tarrington.

"Mrs. Preston," began Coventry, "I notice that you spoke to my learned friend while he was cross-examining Mr. Brown. I don't want to know what you said, but no doubt you heard him ask Mr. Brown if he broke into Mr. Amberley's room?"

"Yes, I heard him," said Anne.

"And were you very relieved when you heard Mr. Brown say 'No'?"

"Why should I have been relieved?"

"Were you?"

"Of course not."

"If Mr. Brown had broken into Mr. Amberley's room, he might have found a photograph of you there, mightn't he?"

"Certainly not."

"A photograph in quite a compromising position?"

"No," said Anne.

"Would you consider this a photograph of you in a compromising position, Mrs. Preston? Let me have it, please, Mr. Ringmer."

Mr. Ringmer handed Coventry the photograph. He glanced at it for rather longer than was necessary, then he handed it to the usher, who took it to Anne.

"The liar!" said Anne to herself, but loud enough to be heard.

"What did you say?" asked Coventry.

"Nothing," said Anne.

"You did, madam," said the judge, "you said 'The liar.' "

"It was a slip. I'm sorry, my lord," said Anne.

"You meant Mr. Brown, didn't you?" asked the judge. "You meant he was a liar for saying he hadn't broken into Mr. Amberley's room."

Anne didn't answer.

"That's right, isn't it?" said the judge.

Anne said nothing but nodded slightly.

"Let me see the photograph."

The usher took the photograph to the judge.

"Mrs. Preston," said the judge when he had looked at it, "you called Mr. Brown a liar for saying he hadn't taken this photograph from Mr. Amberley's room when he had?"

Anne nodded.

"You'd better see the photograph, Mr. Tarrington."

The usher took it to Tarrington. At that stage Amberley got up and said loudly:

"But I've never taken a photograph of her in my life, my lord."

"Silence," said the usher.

The judge looked sharply at Amberley and then said:

"You may recall Mr. Amberley, Mr. Tarrington, if you want—in a moment."

"Thank you, my lord," said Tarrington.

"Mr. Brown wasn't lying as a matter of fact, Mrs. Preston," said Coventry. "It was a colleague of his who got the photograph."

"You're all a lot of bloody tricksters," said Anne wildly.

"I'm sorry, Mrs. Preston. I really am," and it sounded

as if Coventry really meant it. "No more questions," he added.

"You may leave the box, madam," said the judge. "Now, Mr. Amberley."

Anne shook her head resignedly at Amberley as she left the witness box. Amberley went hurriedly into it.

"Now, Mr. Amberley," said Tarrington, "what have you to say about this?"

"I'm sorry I shouted out, my lord," he said, "but I was so taken aback."

"You swear you've never taken a photograph of Mrs. Preston?" asked the judge.

"Only one."

"But you shouted out that you'd never taken one," said Tarrington.

"Not one like this. Never. But I'd forgotten that I did take a snap of her at the races. Fully dressed."

Tarrington sat down and Coventry rose to cross-examine.

"Mr. Amberley," he said, "if Mr. Brown's colleague found this photograph in your room, can you account for it?"

"No, I can't."

"Mrs. Preston seems to think you took it, doesn't she?"

"I don't understand it."

"It is a photograph of her, isn't it?"

"Obviously."

"Someone must have taken it."

"Of course."

"You had the opportunity, didn't you?"

"The opportunity? Yes, I suppose I had."

"And you took advantage of it, didn't you, Mr. Amberley? You wanted something to remind you of the occasion, didn't you?"

"That isn't true. There wasn't an occasion—as you call it."

"This is a photograph of the woman you kissed, isn't it?"

"You know it is."

Coventry stopped for a minute or two and then went on with a slight degree of menace in his voice.

"D'you know what a polaroid camera is?" he asked.

"Yes."

"It's convenient for anyone who wants to take a certain kind of photograph, isn't it?"

"You mean because you don't have to take the films to be developed and printed?"

"Exactly. The camera does it all. You can have the finished product within a minute."

"Yes, I know."

"Have you a polaroid camera?"

"Well, yes, I have."

"This photograph is taken with one, isn't it?"

"It could be."

"It's a photograph of the woman you said you'd have liked to sleep with, isn't it?"

"I've said so," said Amberley in a slightly irritated tone.

"If you had slept with her, this photograph would have been a pleasant reminder, wouldn't it?"

"There's nothing indecent about the photograph."

"I didn't say it was indecent. I said it would be a pleasant reminder. All the more pleasant for not being indecent."

"What d'you expect me to say to that?"

"His lordship expects you to answer the truth. If you had slept with Mrs. Preston, this photograph of her sitting on the bed in her underclothes would have been a pleasant reminder, wouldn't it?"

"As it never happened, it wouldn't have reminded me of anything," said Amberley.

"But if it *had* happened, it would have reminded you—and most pleasantly?"

"It would have reminded me of Mrs. Preston."

"On a bed?"

"On a bed!" said Amberley loudly and angrily.

"Thank you, Mr. Amberley," said Coventry, "that is all I wish to ask."

20 Collapse

Amberley left the witness box and sat down by Mr. Shuttle.

"I must speak to you outside," he said.

"Come along then," said Mr. Shuttle and they left the Court.

"I simply don't understand this," said Amberley when they were in the corridor.

Mr. Shuttle said nothing.

"Don't you believe what I say?" asked Amberley.

"It doesn't matter what I believe," said Mr. Shuttle. "It's what the judge thinks matters."

"Well, do you think he believes me?"

"Quite frankly," said Mr. Shuttle, "I don't see how he can."

"Why d'you say that?"

"Well," said Mr. Shuttle, "there's no doubt someone took a photograph of Mrs. Preston on a bed in her underclothes. And, if she in effect admits it was you, as she does, how can you expect the judge to believe you when you said it wasn't?"

"Then we're going to lose?"

"No case is lost till it's over," said Mr. Shuttle, "but I'm afraid it looks very like it."

"I just can't understand it."

At that moment Anne came out, followed by Mr. Ringmer, Mr. Brown, and Moriarty. Amberley went straight up to Anne but before he could speak Mr. Ringmer intervened.

"The judge says that we must not let the witnesses speak to each other and he relies on you and me, Shuttle, to see that they don't."

"What's all this in aid of?" asked Mr. Shuttle.

"I've no idea," said Mr. Ringmer, "but he's called Mrs. Amberley into the witness box again and sent all the other witnesses outside."

"How very odd," said Mr. Shuttle.

"Can't I say anything to Mrs. Preston?" asked Amberley.

"I'm afraid not," said Mr. Shuttle. "You heard what Mr. Ringmer said."

Meanwhile Anne had walked up the corridor about ten or fifteen yards away from the others.

Inside the Court Jane had gone into the witness box. The judge reminded her that she was still on oath and said that he was sorry to trouble her again. Would she prefer to sit down? Jane preferred to stand.

"You look a little worried," said the judge.

"Well, I am, my lord. It's natural really," said Jane.

"You're worried about the case?"

"Yes, my lord."

"Very natural. Is it because you're very anxious to get rid of your husband or because there's someone else you want to marry?"

"I don't really know what to say," said Jane.

"Mrs. Preston said that she thought you'd got someone else lined up—as she put it . . ."

"That woman would say anything."

"But you don't know her, do you? As I understood your evidence, all you could tell us was that you had a row with your husband and he left you, and then you put the matter into Mr. Brown's hands."

"Yes, my lord."

"I suppose you feel Mrs. Preston would say anything, because of what you've heard about her in this case?"

"That's exactly it, my lord."

"In short, you've heard she's a bad lot?"

"Very, my lord," said Jane.

"And has probably committed adultery with your husband many more times than Mr. Brown has found out?"

"I feel sure of it, my lord."

"So that your husband knows her a good deal more than he's admitted?"

"I'm sure of it, my lord."

"I wonder if you could tell me something rather personal, Mrs. Amberley? Many of us have some distinguishing marks on our bodies—a mole or a scar, or something of that kind. Has your husband?"

"My husband? I don't quite understand, my lord."

"It's quite simple, Mrs. Amberley. Has your husband a birthmark?" He paused and Jane shook her head. "A rather prominent mole?" Jane shook her head again. "A scar perhaps?"

"Oh, I see, my lord. Yes, he has a scar. A rather large appendix scar. It was an awkward operation."

"I see," said the judge. "Just two other questions, Mrs. Amberley. You are a wealthy woman?"

"I suppose you might say so, my lord."

"And you want this divorce very much?"

"Yes, my lord. I do."

"Thank you, Mrs. Amberley. Now I'd like to see Mrs. Preston in the box again, please. I haven't much to ask."

The usher went out to fetch Anne.

"Why am I wanted again?" asked Anne.

"His lordship's orders," said the usher.

"But it's not fair."

"Come along, please, madam."

Anne walked to where Mr. Shuttle was standing.

"Mr. Shuttle," she said, "can't you stop this? It's torture. The judge wants me in the witness box again. Have I got to go?"

"I'm afraid so, Mrs. Preston," said Mr. Shuttle.

"Suppose I refuse?"

"Please don't do that. It wouldn't be in your interest or Mr. Amberley's."

"Leave me to be the judge of that please," said Anne. "What would happen if I refuse?"

"I'm afraid the judge would probably send you to prison."

"How long for?"

"I can't possibly say, but probably until you agreed to give evidence."

"D'you mean to say," said Anne, "that he could keep me in prison until I agreed to go into the box again?"

"I'm afraid so," said Mr. Shuttle.

"But then I'd gain nothing at all from going to prison?"

"Nothing whatever," said Mr. Shuttle. "On the contrary. I repeat, it's in your own interest to do what the judge has asked."

"Well, I shall protest," said Anne.

"Come along, please, madam," said the usher. "The judge is waiting for you."

"I should be careful how you protest, Mrs. Preston," said Mr. Shuttle. "You don't want to get into trouble again."

"It's all a bloody shame," said Anne and burst into tears. "All right, I'll come," she almost shouted to the usher. She went in with him and Mr. Shuttle followed leaving Mr. Ringmer to keep his eye on the witnesses.

As she went into the Court she dabbed at her eyes with a handkerchief.

"Come into the witness box, please, Mrs. Preston," said the judge.

"It isn't fair," said Anne tearfully. "How many more times? Why should they persecute me like this, my lord? Can't I appeal to you for help? Won't you stop them? I've had as much as I can stand."

"I'm afraid it's I who want you back for a moment," said the judge. "Counsel didn't ask for you this time. I shan't keep you long."

"What difference does it make?" said Anne as she stepped into the witness box. "I don't believe anyone's ever been backwards and forwards into the witness box like this. I tell you I can't stand any more of it."

"Calm yourself, madam," said the judge.

"Calm yourself—calm yourself! How can I? I've done no more than thousands of other women have done. Why should I be persecuted like this? Most people don't go to court at all. I've had enough. All right, I slept with him, if that's what you want. But he's good and kind and decent and he needed some comfort after what he'd had to put up with with her."

The judge nodded to Coventry, who rose.

"Mrs. Preston," he said, "do you then admit you've committed adultery with Mr. Amberley?"

"Haven't I just said so?" said Anne. "How many more times do you lawyers want it? In the hotel, in the car, in my flat—is that what you want? Well, you can have the lot—and there are plenty more where they come from. And I hope they choke you. May I go now, please?"

"Very well," said the judge. "Just wait in the corridor, please."

Anne stumbled out of the witness box and out of the door weeping hysterically.

As soon as she had gone, Coventry said:

"Well, my lord, I don't know if my learned friend wishes to address you, but, if he doesn't, on that evidence I would ask for a decree *nisi*."

"What do you say, Mr. Tarrington?" said the judge.

"I must consult both my clients," said Tarrington, "before I submit to any such order."

"Quite so," said the judge. "But, before you do, I think I'd like to have a word with you both privately. At the moment I'm sharing my room with another judge. So I think we'll stay here. Clear the Court, please, usher."

Everyone left the Court except the judge and counsel.

21 Again Why Not?

Outside the Court Mr. Shuttle went straight to Amberley and told him what had happened.

"I can't believe it," he said.

"I'm afraid it happened," said Mr. Shuttle.

"Can I speak to her?" said Amberley.

"Not at the moment," said Mr. Shuttle. "Not till the case is over."

"But from what you tell me, it is over," said Amberley.

"I'm afraid it almost is," said Mr. Shuttle. "But till judgment has been given the judge said the witnesses were not to talk to each other."

"Well, I tell you I've never committed adultery," said Amberley. "You don't believe me, I suppose?"

"I'd rather not answer," said Mr. Shuttle.

"I'd rather you did," said Amberley.

"Well, if you must have it," said Mr. Shuttle, "I don't. I can't."

"Is there anything I've said myself that makes you disbelieve me?"

"No, I can't say there is."

"Then it's entirely what Anne has said."

"Yes, I suppose it is," said Mr. Shuttle.

"Why believe her and not me?" asked Amberley.

"Really, Mr. Amberley," said Mr. Shuttle, "this isn't a case like that. It's not as if she were on the one side and you were on the other. She's very fond of you. Her very last words were that you were kind and decent."

"She must have had a brainstorm," said Amberley.

"She's certainly distressed," said Mr. Shuttle. "But she appeared to be perfectly normal mentally, but, if you like, I'll speak to her."

"Yes," said Amberley, "I wish you would."

"Very well," said Mr. Shuttle, "I'll go and have a word with her."

Meantime the judge had taken off his wig and come down to the well of the Court.

"Make yourselves at home," he said. "Smoke, if you want to. I'm going to."

He took out a pipe and lit it, while Tarrington and Coventry took cigarettes.

"I think I'll walk around a bit," he said. "One gets a bit stiff sitting up there all the time."

He walked around the Court and then paused at the "No Smoking" sign. "I wonder they don't put 'Please do not spit' as well. I'll be glad when they build some decent courts for us. What was this?"

"It was one of the associates' rooms, I think, judge," said Coventry.

"Oh, well, houses must come first," said the judge. "And

hospitals. But I don't see why offices should. How are you both?"

"Well, thank you, judge," said Coventry, "and you?"

"Mustn't grumble," said the judge. "But I do. Gout—and my father was a teetotaler, the old fool. Well, now, this is a rum do."

"I must say I didn't expect it to come out as it did," said Coventry.

"If you ask me, it hasn't come out," said the judge. "Well, not in the way you mean. I don't believe Mrs. Preston ever committed adultery with Mr. Amberley."

"What!" said Coventry and Tarrington together.

"But she's admitted it, judge," added Coventry.

"I know."

"I'm as much in the dark as Coventry, judge," said Tarrington.

"I was in the dark for some time," said the judge. "But I don't think I am now. What d'you think of Amberley as a witness?"

"I must admit he's pretty good," said Coventry.

"If it weren't for Mrs. Preston's evidence—you'd be inclined to believe him, wouldn't you?" said the judge.

"Yes—I think I should."

"But she sinks him like a stone."

"That's exactly what I said, judge," said Coventry and, looking at Tarrington for confirmation, added, "isn't it?"

"It's odd," said the judge, "that a man can appear so transparently honest—and yet be a thumping liar."

"It happens, judge," said Coventry.

"Yes, it does occasionally, but I can't believe it in this case. I think I have the solution. You're not going to like it—"

Suddenly a thought came to Coventry.

"D'you mean—" he began.

"Yes."

"May I be let into the secret, judge?" asked Tarrington.

"You may," said the judge. "Mrs. Amberley wants a divorce. That's one thing that is plain."

"Quite."

"How's she to get one if Amberley won't oblige? One way is to get a woman who'll swear she has committed adultery with him and an inquiry agent to corroborate her. That's all right if they do commit adultery, of course. But suppose they don't. The woman comes along and falsely admits her guilt. The husband denies it. If he's telling the truth, and the woman is lying, she can usually be cross-examined into a cocked hat. I've seen some of these put-up jobs, and they're very difficult to bring off. Very difficult indeed. But suppose, instead, you get the woman to deny that she's committed adultery, to appear to fight like a tigress, and then in the end to allow herself to be blown to bits. The fact that she's fought the case makes it appear that she must be genuine, and when she collapses she brings the innocent husband down with her. It's a certainty unless the conspiracy is realized—a conspiracy which, unless I'm much mistaken, will land your client, Coventry, and one of yours, Tarrington, at the Old Bailey along with Mr. Brown."

"What led you to it, judge?" asked Coventry.

"Well, Amberley made me wonder from the start. The contrast between him and the woman. Why should she be such a bad witness, if they're innocent? And then his outburst over the photograph made me feel sure. It had the ring of truth about it."

"So you did take notice of a witness's demeanor outside the witness box?"

"Quite right. It's the first time. And you two have been used like marionettes. Very artistically, I must say. It must have looked genuine with the passport, the breaking in, the torn letter, and all the rest of it. And even at the end she keeps it up by saying what a good fellow Amberley is. That must be a genuine confession, mustn't it? But it isn't."

"But if she hadn't been recalled she wouldn't have had a chance to make her admission," said Coventry.

"But she'd done it already over the photograph. In effect she admitted Amberley had taken it. If I believed that I was bound to find against them. This last performance was merely painting the lily."

"But why should she risk being prosecuted for perjury?"

"Because they never are, any more than a thief who at first swears he's not guilty and later admits it. And anyway people don't expect to be found out. Why should they be? Neither of you suspected anything. The chances were that nobody would."

"How can you be sure you're right, judge? Where's the proof?"

"I think a few more questions to Mrs. Preston will satisfy you. I'm satisfied already. I'll tell you another thing. This is only a hunch, but I don't believe she was ever charged with indecency years ago in a car. I believe that's just an invention. D'you see the effect of it? She was acquitted. So no one's going to bother to try to turn up the proceedings. But it cast an unhealthy flavor about her—even though she was acquitted. As you pointed out, it was a very odd coincidence. So I'll ask her about that first."

"That's consistent with my instructions. I was only told

about it vaguely. As you remember, I had to feel my way very, very gently about it."

"Shall we have them back? Let's clear the smoke away first."

Outside in the corridor Mr. Shuttle was talking to Amberley again.

"I'm afraid she's perfectly normal," he said.

"But did she say it again to you?" asked Amberley.

"She said she was very sorry to let you and me down but she'd come to the end of her tether and couldn't stand any more."

"I know what it is," said Amberley. "It's third-degree stuff in open court. They've just broken the poor girl down. She admits it, not because it's true but because they've broken down her resistance. Of course, that's what it is. Please tell Mr. Tarrington about this. I know I'm right. She's just too tired to resist any longer. It's the same thing with physical torture. This has been mental torture. Most people have their breaking point, and she'd say anything now rather than have to fight any more. Poor girl. I don't blame her after what she's gone through. But we can get medical evidence about this. We'll be able to prove she wasn't herself when she said what she did."

"Well," said Mr. Shuttle, "I've never known an innocent person break down like this. But of course it's possible and I'll certainly tell Mr. Tarrington what you say."

At that moment the usher came out.

"The Court is open," he said. "Come in, please."

Meanwhile the judge and counsel had done their best to clear away the smoke and, duly robed, were sitting in their places.

"I'm very sorry, Mrs. Preston," said the judge, "but I'm

afraid I'd like you to come back into the witness box."

"Me?" said Anne.

"Yes, please," said the judge.

"After what I've said?"

"Yes, I'm afraid so, but it won't be for long."

Anne walked slowly to the witness box.

"I shan't keep you long," said the judge.

Amberley whispered to Mr. Shuttle.

"Tell Tarrington what I've said. It's not fair to put her through any more."

Mr. Shuttle spoke to Tarrington, who got up.

"Would you forgive me, my lord, if before you ask Mrs. Preston any more questions I have a word with Mr. Amberley and my professional client?"

"Very well," said the judge. "You'd better go outside but don't be too long, please."

Tarrington, Amberley, and Mr. Shuttle went out.

"You must stop this," said Amberley. "She may have a nervous breakdown."

"I don't follow," said Tarrington.

"Those admissions she made are simply the result of a breakdown. This cross-examination has pretty well killed her. She knows as well as I do that we haven't slept together. She's simply been forced to admit it. If the judge goes on at her any more it might really injure her health."

"Mr. Amberley," said Tarrington, "I think you're going to get a surprise."

"A surprise?"

"Yes. You'd never met Mrs. Preston till after you'd left your wife, had you?"

"No."

"And then one day you got talking to her while you were

both in the bar of the hotel where you were staying."

"That's right. What's that got to do with it?" asked Amberley.

"Well, I'm in rather a difficulty because I'm appearing for you both," said Tarrington, "but I don't think I'll have to do much more in this case."

"But you've got to," said Amberley. "You've got to explain to the judge what's happened and get an adjournment. I tell you we're both absolutely innocent."

"I believe you are," said Tarrington.

"You believe *I* am?" queried Amberley. "But, if I am, we both are."

"In a way, yes," said Tarrington, "but in another way no. Come into court and listen. I think you're going to be relieved, but, as you're still fond of Mrs. Preston, you won't be extremely pleased."

"I don't know what on earth you're talking about," said Amberley.

"How could you?" said Tarrington. "But come back into court and I think you will."

Tarrington went in followed by Mr. Shuttle and a very puzzled Amberley.

"I'm sorry to have delayed your lordship," said Tarrington.

"Now, Mrs. Preston," said the judge. "I wonder if you would help us about one thing. I'm sorry to raise the matter again. What was the Court where you were acquitted thirteen years ago?"

"The court, my lord?"

"Yes, the name of the court."

"The name?" repeated Anne.

"Yes, the name."

Anne hesitated. Then:

"I can't remember," she said.

"Try and think," said the judge. "You can't have been in so many courts in your life."

Anne said nothing.

"Well, what county was it in?" asked the judge.

"I simply can't remember," said Anne.

At that moment Amberley stood up.

"Stop it, please, my lord," he said. "She can't stand any more. If you go on like this she won't be able to remember her own name. She's completely broken down."

"Silence," said the usher.

"That's all right," said the judge. "No, Mr. Amberley, I don't think Mrs. Preston has completely broken down. Have you, madam?"

"I'm very upset," said Anne.

"Well, of course," said the judge. "But you're well enough to answer a few more questions?"

"Why have I got to?"

"Because I want you to. It will take only a few minutes. Now about this court, perhaps you've tried to blot the whole thing out of your memory, and that's why you can't remember anything about it."

"To be perfectly truthful," said Anne, "that is the case."

"To be perfectly truthful," repeated the judge. "Humph. Well, I do believe you don't know which court it was in. Why didn't you go a bit further and forget it had happened, Mrs. Preston? You'd have liked to, I suppose?"

"Yes, my lord."

"A great pity you didn't succeed. Well, I won't ask any more about that then. Sit down, Mr. Amberley, I'm not going to ill-treat Mrs. Preston, but there's just a little more

I must ask her. Would you like to sit down, madam?"

"No, thank you."

"Mr. Amberley thinks that you've admitted adultery simply because you've been bullied by counsel. Is that right, Mr. Amberley?"

"Yes, my lord, it is. I'm not criticizing Mr. Coventry. He's got his job to do, but it's the effect it's had on her."

"In other words," said the judge to Anne, "Mr. Amberley is saying that your confession of adultery is a false one. Is it?"

Anne shook her head.

"Are you sure?" said the judge.

Anne shook her head again.

Even Amberley was surprised, so surprised that he sat down.

"Well, Mrs. Preston," continued the judge, "d'you know the reason why I want you to come back into the witness box?"

"No, my lord."

"No idea at all?"

"No, my lord."

"Well," said the judge quietly but very firmly, "you will know in a minute."

Anne looked at him sharply and then started to pale.

"You've said that Mrs. Amberley wants to torture you. You don't think I do, I hope."

"Oh, no, my lord."

"I'm glad of that because I have some very awkward questions to ask you."

"Awkward, my lord?" said Anne, by this time looking very pale indeed.

"The most awkward you can think of," said the judge.

He paused and then went on: "Mrs. Preston, you have admitted adultery with Mr. Amberley on many occasions. What do you think is the most awkward question I could ask you?"

"I don't understand, my lord."

"I think you do. I could ask you to describe his body. That was the one thing it wasn't necessary for Mr. Brown or Mrs. Amberley to tell you about. You were going to deny adultery until the very end. So what did you have to know about his body?"

Anne sat down.

"He may have a big appendix scar on it—but then he may not. He may have a very large mole somewhere—but then he may not. He may have—need I go on? Would you risk answering any such question, Mrs. Preston—would you?"

"No—my lord," said Anne faintly.

"Well, Mrs. Preston, if you really have slept with Mr. Amberley, why not? Why not?"